# About the Author

Throughout his career in teaching and education consultancy, Paul has developed a fascination with the amazing life stories of those who have gone before us. Women and men facing ever changing social norms and life's challenges, within the timeframe of where and when they lived. His passions include genealogy and travel, resulting in his books being based in places visited and fondly remembered. Actively engaged in community affairs, being Rotary International district governor and chair of his state's Duke of Edinburgh scheme, he has had the opportunity to interact with and learn from a range of people.

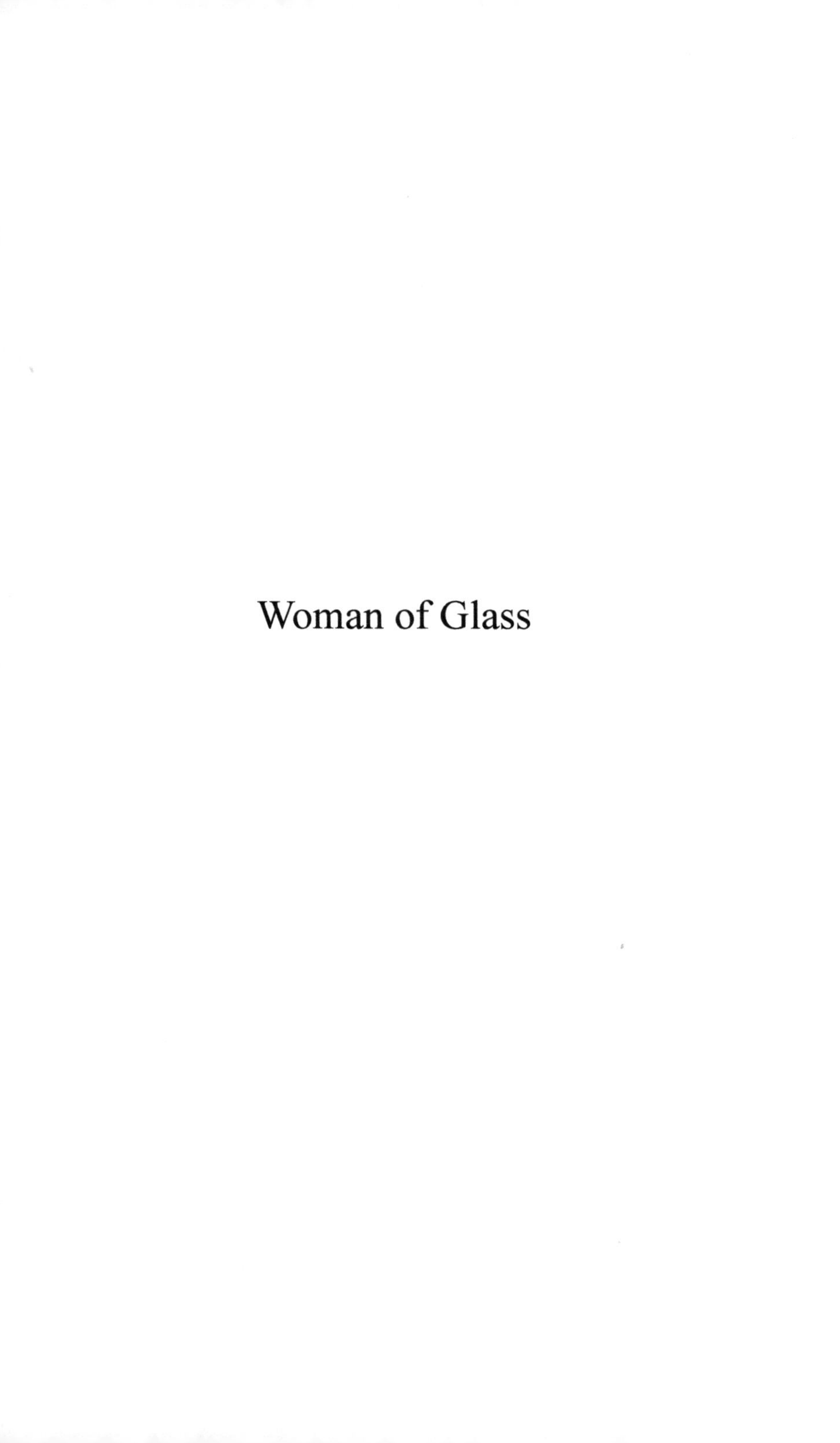

Woman of Glass

# Paul Erickson

---

# Woman of Glass

Vanguard Press

Dedicated to Christina, an amazing woman, the matriarch of a pioneering family in the Australian bottle making industry. Unfortunately like so many women before and after her, Christina did not get the credit or recognition she deserved. Though not a household name, her story deserves to be told.

# Prologue: 1855

John was shocked when he opened the door. His son stood in stockinged feet, a gash over his left eye. Christina was beside him, her bonnet missing, and one sleeve of her dress torn, a thin line of blood running over her ice white shoulder.

This was not the first intimidation the family had endured. John's wife had been threatened by a passerby while standing outside their home and two weeks earlier a large cobble stone had been thrown, smashing the glass in John's workshop window.

John and Jean had been talking about a move for several months, but it was originally driven by the thought of providing better educational and employment opportunities for their children. This had now changed to fear. John realised the stance he had taken, and the high profile he and his family had in the Wick community had become a threat to both himself and his children. The decision was made, the family commenced packing their trunks for the move to Edinburgh.

For Christina this was the beginning of a new life. Forced to leave her Scottish homeland, Christina accepts a position of governess and eventually wife of an English glassmaker. At his beckoning, she endures the dangers associated with the voyage to the colony of New South Wales where she struggled to adapt to a totally different set of norms in a harsh environment. She often felt alone, as her husband becomes preoccupied with struggling business ventures. Through fire, bankruptcies and family conflict she is forced to take control of the company becoming the matriarch of a fledgling industry.

While raising her thirteen children she actively questions and challenges the barriers and limitations that society had placed on her gender.

The story of one of the many female pioneers who helped develop new industries and changed the inequality experienced by women in colonial Australia.

# Chapter 1

The house stood on the high side of High Street, overlooking the Wick River. Robert Grant had built it in the early 1830s and it was now the third bluestone house he owned. This one consisted of three storeys, a shop front and workspace on the ground floor, living area on the first and the attic with small bay windows, the attic floor space divided into small bedrooms suitable for children or servants. The grey slate roof matched the houses on either side. Robert was pleased when his newlywed daughter, Jean, and son-in-law, John Fraser, had opted to settle in Wick and rent the house, allowing John to set up his own shoe making business.

John was a Highland boy but had done his apprenticeship in Inverness. Jean had met him there while attending a Ceilidh accompanied by her Sinclair cousins, with whom she was staying. Being introduced by mutual friends, Jean and John had danced a strathspey, with its slower and statelier steps, followed by a faster reel then a lively jig. The music had been loud and exhilarating with bagpipes, fiddles and the Clarsach Harp filling the night air.

Sitting over supper, their immediate bond could be seen by all. John, in an attempt to impress Jean, had commented on her green, low, square-toed satin slippers saying he would be pleased to make her others in any colour she wanted.

The Fraser's loved their new home, a quiet fishing community, free from noise and uproar, a community based on close family ties and heritage. The main industry was a small fishing fleet and three rope making factories that employed seventy-five men. Since the late 1740s the major source of income in the area had been the linen spinning. This was a cottage industry that could be found in nearly every home. As a small community, the Frasers' knew all their neighbours and most of the business people in their self-sufficient community. In such an environment children were free to roam, front doors were never locked and it was safe to walk the streets day and night. However, impending rapid growth would mean prosperity for some but for others, the destruction of their beliefs about what was important in their world. Harsh reality was to clash with the hopes and idealism of residents of this tiny community. Their quaint town was about to become Europe's "Herringopolis."

Wick lies at the end of a triangular bay opening onto the North Sea, an estuary of the Wick River in northwest Scotland. The term Wick is of Scandinavian origins and signifies an opening, appropriate in a description of the town's location. Originally it had been a Norwegian colony on the North Sea, consisting of a few thatched cottages, acting as a small trading post. Over time, it had developed into a drab looking settlement of grey shores and grey houses, the area of shallow poor-quality soil, almost treeless. Where trees did grow they were oddly shaped, stunted and twisted by the fierce salty winds. To the visitor it was a melancholy place that could easily cause a feeling of pensive sadness of spirit. Robert Louis Stevenson, while visiting his uncle who lived in Wick, would call it, 'One of the meanest of man's towns, on the baldest of God's bays.'

However, to John's daughter Christina and the Fraser family this was home. The only access to the south, at the beginning of the 19th century, was a foot bridge over the Wick River consisting of eleven pillars, built of loose stone, with timber laid over them. It was maintained by the families living to the south to allow access to the church in Wick. This Old Parish Church in High Street, a Church of Scotland, had been built in the 1820s by John Henry of Edinburgh. Christina's grandfather, Robert Grant, a stone mason, had been employed in its construction. It was the Fraser's family church, and each Sunday Christina would sit in their hard wooden pew, an enclosed box, housed in this Gothic structure. It was constructed of blue flag stone with soft freestone at the corners, doors, windows and the spire. The church had a single stage tower, slate roof and spacious galleried interior. In the graveyard to the east stood the remains of the Sinclair Aisle, part of the old parish kirk dedicated to St Fergus and built around 1570. St Fergus or Fergustian, had been an Irish bishop who worked in Scotland as a missionary. Near the corner of the old church was the original well, also dedicated to St Fergus.

John Fraser Junior, Christina's brother, who was five years older, liked to tease and trick his siblings, as many older brothers do. Thus, to Christina, the Sinclair Aisle was a scary place, built of dark, locally quarried stone and John had told her of evil ghosts that rose from a large vault below that contained a sealed lead lined coffin. According to John, 'It was the body of John Garrow, Master of Caithness that lies within.'

Garrow had been involved in a siege of Castle Dornoch and when the Murray family capitulated, they had handed over three hostages. These innocents were beheaded, their souls now seeking revenge on the Sutherland and Sinclair clans. As Christina's mother was a Sinclair, John insisted they would be after her. Christina doubted lots of things John told her but knew there really was a vault, her father had also talked about it.

John also gave accounts of the witches, thrown down the well, screaming to be set free. Though she didn't want to believe him, Christina knew there had been witch trials, their minister had mentioned them in one of his very long sermons. He had talked about the evils of the Witchcraft Act that had remained in law till 1736. As it had been a capital crime in Scotland, those convicted were either strangled or burned at the stake. In reality, Scotland executed five times as many witches, per capita, than anywhere else in Europe. It was estimated that over two thousand five hundred were killed as witches, eighty-four percent women. Even the king, James VI of Scotland, was involved in what the minister referred to as 'Scotland's satanic panic.' During his sermon, the minister had held up a text, *Daemonologie, in Forme of a Dialogue*, that had been written by the king in 1597. It was a study of demonology and the methods used by demons. The minister used it to denounce what he saw to be the current demons, especially the evils of alcoholic spirits and the declining moral standards within their community.

Even as a child, Christina realised that things around her were changing. There were many more strangers wandering the streets and her parents had become far more protective. She was not allowed out of the family home unless accompanied by her parents or eldest brother John. She understood the need for this as she had seen drunken men fighting in the streets, urinating against walls and heard cries of dismay when purses were snatched. She had noticed women walking the streets, chatting to the fishermen then slyly moving into back alleys or one of the rundown buildings that lined the smaller streets near the harbour.

Christina also knew that something had happened to her sister Barbara who was seven years older than her. She had heard her parents talking and thought it had something to do with some strangers trying to drag Barbara into a wagon, when she kicked, screamed and bit one of them she had escaped. Regardless of the reason, except to go with the family to church, Barbara rarely left the house and seemed content working at her loom. John had warned his daughter that there were reports of young women being kidnapped from remote coastal villages and taken into the Highlands or peat moors and forced to marry pig famers or peat cutters. John called it bride kidnapping or marriage by abduction.

Sometimes these were elopements where the couple run away together and seek the consent of their parents later. Often this was a clan issue, one family refusing to marry into another clan. Actually the concept of a honeymoon is a relic of this practice with the husband going into hiding with his captured wife, to avoid the reprisal from relatives. The month of hiding was with the intension that the woman would become pregnant thus not wanting or able to return to her family. Some men also participated in bride snatching to avoid having to pay the asked bride price or bride-dowry. For the reluctant brides they often spent the first month locked in a shed or barn some tied to a post with rope or chain to prevent them from escaping. At least once a day the groom would insist on sexual intercourse, the intention to produce a child. After the lock down period the bride would be taken to her husband's family home where she would be placed under the care of his mother or female relative. The switch, a flexible rod was a common corporal punishment for the slightest infringement of the rules or disobedience.

If the girl failed to become pregnant in a perceived suitable time she might be sold on as a factory or brothel worker in one of England's bigger cities. Here with limited or no pay and no way home the girls became a slave of the new Industrial Revolution.

As most of these weddings were sham, performed by a local with no power or authority, and were not registered, the groom once rid of his bride would start planning another kidnapping, hopefully this time the girl would be more fertile.

# Chapter 2

Though Christina's father would not have approved, as he considered witches, fairies and folklore blasphemous, it was her grandmother Barbara Sinclair, who would tell the children imaginative stories based on Scottish folklore. Barbara had been born in Dunnet on the north coast of Caithness and moved to Wick when she married Robert Grant. Robert Grant's clan was a Highland clan, and one that could trace their heritage as far back as the ninth century and Kenneth MacAlpine, king of Scotland. The Grants had considerable influence over the northeast of Scotland and had been strong supporters of William Wallace. Wallace was a Scottish knight who had been a leader in the First War of Scottish Independence.

Barbara would refer to the good fairies and the wicked wichts. While walking with her grandchildren along the cliffs, she would point to moving shapes in the sea,

'Ashrays, sea ghosts, their bodies translucent and hard to see.'

Near the river she talked about the bean-nighe, a small creature, dressed in green with webbed feet, who would drag you into the water if you got too close to the edge. When they slept over at a new villa that Robert had built himself on the escarpment overlooking the planned township of Upper Pulteney, she warned them to be careful of the bodach, a monster spirit who came down the chimney to poke, prod and pinch children who had been naughty, thus encouraging them to always be nice. Another of her tales related to the cù-sìth, a fairy dog that hunted at night in the wastelands. She warned the children about the dangers of being away from the safety of their home after sunset.

It took John many years to realise his grandmother's fables each had a meaning, a life lesson designed to make their lives safer. Her use of anthropomorphism to attribute human traits and emotions to non-human entities would have concerned the children's parents as it had been raised as an issue in their church, originally in reference to the heresy of applying a human form to the Christian God.

When John's father heard him telling his sister about the bean-nighe, he had admonished him.

John had replied, 'It was only to scare her from going too close to the river, she likes to play there and might fall in.'

To his father it was still a lie, but John argued that even in the bible, there were stories with good intention. Their minister at Sabbath School had taught them about parables, Jesus' teaching to explain a particular concept or value. John had already reached an age where he challenged many of the Old Testament stories. He questioned passages like Genesis and the tale of Noah and his Ark and the same with 2 Kings, Jonah and the Whale. He couldn't see much difference between the tale of a whale or one of the ashray.

John loved visiting his grandmother, she usually made him his favourite dinner, cock-a-leekie, chicken stewed with leeks, and also had cake. However, on other visits she would serve his least favourite, haggis. This savoury pudding consisted of sheep's pluck (heart, liver and lung) minced with onion, and suet boiled with oatmeal in a sheep's stomach. Considered a traditional delicacy, he didn't like the nutty texture or the neeps (turnips) that were served with it. Barbara always served it at the family gathering on Burns Nicht. This celebration held on the 25th of January, was a celebration of the life and poetry of the bard, Robert Burns, the author of many Scots poems. Barbara, like many Scots, was proud of his use of the Scottish dialect and his achievements in popularising the Scots language. Unlike her son-in-law, Barbara still served her haggis with whisky while she recited Burns poetry.

When John went to bed, Barbara would softly sing to him  her version of Frere Jacques;
'Frere Jacques
Frere Jacques
Dearthair John,
Dearthair John
Sonnez les matines
Sonnez les matines
Ding dong
Ding dong"

Though she spoke Gaelic to him, Barbara always used French when conversing with his mother. Over time, he had also learned enough French to understand basic conversations and give simple replies. He knew his grandmother could understand English, but she chose not to use it.

Their house was larger and more modern than his parents'. Robert Grant owned the lease to the local quarry, thus when the new harbour and town of Pulteneytown were developed on the south side of the Wick River by the British Fisheries Society, Robert had provided most of the stone and also supervised the building of several civic buildings. Moving to Upper Pulteneytown was the thing to do, for those who could afford it. On the escarpment strong sea breezes carried away the smell of decaying fish that often settle like a dense foul sea mist over lower parts of Wick and Pulteney that was squeezed into an area to the west of the harbour and south of the River Wick. The residents of Upper Pulteneytown had also banded together to employ their own constables, thus crime was less and undesirables were quickly moved on.

While visiting, John would admire his grandmother's sketches that hung in what she referred to as her parlour or withdrawing room, which she used for her own privacy. John estimated the room must measure at least twenty by thirty feet, had two large windows and heavy velvet drapes in an emerald green colour. Towards the centre was a round table with chairs that his grandmother used when serving tea. There were also four very comfortable padded armchairs in striking tones, a tartan of red and green in a Georgian style. John loved curling up in one of these reading a book, especially on cold, wet and windy days, which on the northeast coast of Scotland, was most days. On either side of the fireplace with its carved vegetal designs in stone, stood Barbara's bookcase, overflowing with leather bound books.

Most of Barbara's sketches were of castles and Highland scenes. Each of her drawings came with a story, some of imaginary people others real, but always told to entertain. Two drawings were of castles. The first, Knock Castle, was connected to an ancestor, William Fraser, and the second, Castle Fraser, the lands having come into the hands of the Frasers in 1454 when James II, House of Stewart, took over the estates of the Earl of Mar. James had broken the estates up into smaller baronies and granted them to trusted supporters.

John's grandmother often added on stories about the ghosts and spirits that inhabited each particular castle. In the case of Knock, it was the Green Lady or glaisting, that appeared as a half-woman, half-goat, the goat half disguised by a long flowing green robe. She explained that the ghost could be heard wailing when bad things happened in the castle.

As the second oldest of the Fraser children, he had spent much more time with the Grants and his grandfather had hoped that John would take up a stonemason's apprenticeship with him. John however was more interested sitting with his grandmother, learning the basics of drawing, or reading one of the many leather volumes that were shelved in the drawing room. These included authors like Sir Walter Scott and his books of *Rob Roy* and *Ivanhoe*. There was Daniel Defoe's *Robinson Crusoe* and Henry Fielding's *The History of Tom Jones, a Foundling*. There were several novels by Tobias Smollett including *The Adventures of Roderick Random* and *The Adventures of Peregrine Pickle*.

John was not surprised to find that one shelf contained only novels written by Scottish women. John's grandmother's favourite author was Catherine Sinclair. Besides being related, Barbara loved her imaginative and vivid style of writing. Other members of her extended family had sent her a copy of Catherine's children's book *Holiday House: A Series of Tales* that had been published in 1839. The accompanying letter explained that these were actually the stories Catherine had recited to her niece. This somehow made them even more special. Barbara had been impressed at the book's realistic portrayal of children, who were naturally curious, mischievous and sometimes argumentative. That's what she liked about her own grandchildren, especially John and Christina. Though their father was confined by his religion and convictions, the children had spirit, a willingness to try new things and question anything they didn't understand or felt was wrong. Her daughter Jean use to be like that, but after she married John she had changes. She was not the zealot that her son-in-law was becoming, but had become compliant and acquiescent. She went along with whatever John latest plan or initiative might be. When Barbara had offered to pay for a cook or house cleaner to help her daughter, there was the usual reply.

'John wouldn't like that.'

Barbara didn't feel that John Junior should read all Catherine Sinclair's books as some, like *Modern Accomplishments, or the March of Intellect* and *Modern Society* were more suited to his mother as they were concerned with the education of women and contemporary ideas on morality and happiness. Or at least they use to be when she was growing up.

Barbara had informed John that Catherine had been a deeply religious woman, a relative and person of whom he should be proud as she was a philanthropist, involved in charity work in Edinburgh. Barbara had visited the public water fountain that Catherine had erected at the junction of Lothian Road and Prince Street in Edinburgh.

It was a large and elaborate structure, providing fresh drinking water for both travellers and locals. She also loved animals so had some low-level water troughs constructed for them.

The shelf also contained the works of Susan Ferrier. Barbara was impressed that Susan seemed to create a believable portrait of the Edinburgh in which she lived. Barbara particularly liked the fact that distinctive Scottish words and phrases were included in her books. She was aware that many leading intellectuals, and those considered upper class, were anxious to rid what they called "Scotticisms" such as "cou'd na be fashed" (couldn't be bothered). As a proud Scot, this was one of the reasons Barbara generally refused to talk in English.

There were two of Ferrier's books that Barbara had recommended to John. The first, *Destiny,* about the laird of Glenroy, who despite its defects, clung to the old clan system, refusing to enter the modern world, and the terrible consequences on the lives of his family. The second recommendation was *Inheritance*, a tale of a young heroine arriving at a

Highland estate to take up her inheritance but finds herself in the middle of an odd collection of humorous and eccentric characters. Like her folklore tales, Barbara felt these two books both had strong moral lessons to be learnt about the changing face of Scotland.

Two other authors were also represented in Barbara's collection, Elizabeth Hamilton and Mary Brunton. Like Sinclair and Ferrier, these authors wrote about the Scottish landscape, cultures, and challenges in Scottish society. They were writing during the French-Revolutionary era, a period of rapid political and social change when controversy over education and the rights of women was being expressed in Britain. Besides some leather-bound volumes of their work, Barbara had copies that had been repackaged for a different audience. Hamilton's book *The Cottagers of Glenburnie* was expensive, thus read mainly by middle-class, well-educated readers. Barbara had obtained a copy of the book when published as a series called *The Girl's Own Library*. These cheaper booklets were designed to be read by poorer people who lived in the cottages like those in her book. She had also purchased a copy of these for Christina, as from an early age, her granddaughter had demonstrated a quick mind and eagerness to learn

# Chapter 3

Links between Wick and the outside world had slowly improved when a three arch stone bridge was built at Wick to give horse and wagon access between the two sides of the river. At the same time, the Highland Roads Act allowed that the Parliamentary road which ran from Inverness, a city on the east coast, to Thurso, a town on the northeast coast, be extended. This included a grant of twenty thousand pounds towards roads and bridges in the Highlands. The extension being from the Ord, a granite mass and headland on the boundary of the counties of Sutherland and Caithness, to Wick and then to Thurso.

John had publicly questioned the value of these changes for the common folk. As they were built as toll roads to recoup some of the maintenance costs, most locals still chose to use the rough and winding country lanes. In 1818, the mail coach, which was already running between Inverness and Tain a town forty-two miles north of Inverness, was extended to Wick and Thurso. This offered better communication between Wick and the south of Scotland but also increased the outside interest in the commercial opportunities that a rich sea harvest might provide. However, the north mail coach and other wagons still struggled during the winter months when snow covered their Highland paths, in some places up to fifteen feet deep. As Wick was on the coast, there was less snow than the Highlands, but winter still meant frozen soils, black ice and ground frost. In very cold winters the sea also froze, preventing ships from entering the harbour.

To Christina, Wick was a place of rugged beauty, a raw place of a big starlit sky and dramatic light. The exposed coastline constantly being battered by cold black southerly winds, an area of low sunshine levels. On the negative side, in the herring season the streets were full of Highland fishers, lumpy, smelly men that Christina avoided. To the south of the town, the skyline was dominated by spectacular coastal scenery with huge black rugged cliffs, gouged by great black chasms with deep green pools below. The small sheep farms that did exist, required the farmers to also be fishermen in order to make an adequate living. Others supplemented their livelihoods by digging for peat moss, decayed vegetable matter, cut in the summer for fuel. This was made additionally important due to the almost total absence of timber that could be cut for firewood.

The town of Wick, which was becoming the main centre for herring fishing was a regular host to a seasonal population, greatly outnumbering the local inhabitants. The 1790s had seen the British Fisheries Society investigate the prospect of building a harbour and a new fishing village on the southern bank of the Wick River. The land to be developed was acquired from Sir Benjamin Dunbar in 1803 and the architect Thomas Telford was commissioned to build the harbour. Telford was well-known for his construction of canals, city water supplies, and the rebuilding of the London Bridge.

Records showed the fishery in 1818 consisted of four hundred and eighty-two boats with around two thousand seven hundred fishermen, one thousand six hundred gutting women and three hundred coopers. By 1857, a letter from the chairman of the House of Commons Committee on Harbours of Refuge, claimed the Wick area had one thousand one hundred boats with six thousand six hundred fishermen, of which only six hundred actually resided permanently in Wick.

During this time, drunkenness and crime was rife, men were forced to live in sheds, barns or stacked in small rooms, sleeping in shifts on hammocks. Hygiene was very poor and epidemics such a cholera and typhoid seemed to break out each season. There had been reports of local women being assaulted and an increase in property theft. As a result, Christina's father had felt the need to install wooden shutters on their house, and after his day of work all doors would be bolted.

Much to the disgust of the Frasers, by the 1840s the town boasted forty-one licensed premises, twenty in Wick and twenty-one in Pulteneytown, and it was estimated that more than five hundred gallons of whisky were being consumed in and around Wick, every week. Life in Wick now revolved around herring and whisky causing Christina's father John, to worry about the futures of his children. Like Pulteneytown, the local distillery that was established had also been named after Sir William Pulteney, 5th Baronet, a landowner and politician who sat in the House of Commons. He was reputed at the time, to be the wealthiest man in Great Britain.

The distillery had been set up in 1826 and was the most northerly on the Scottish mainland. At the time, the lack of roads and bridges over the Wick River made it quite inaccessible except by sea. Barley was brought in by ship, and the whisky was shipped out the same way. In the herring season many of the distillery workers were also fishermen.

Slowly other industries grew including boatbuilding, rope making and net making. A small iron foundry was founded but was principally concerned with manufacturing items connected with the fishing industry. The town also had a brewery, sawmill and grain mill. With the growth of population Wick had become a market centre for produce from the surrounding region. Weekly markets were held on Friday which Christina's mother found useful both to purchase fresh produce but also to sell some of the clothing items she made from the linen she and her daughter had woven.

# Chapter 4

When Christina Fraser was born in 1842, the township of Wick was a community of around one thousand three hundred people. She was the fourth Fraser child to be born in the High Street home. Her father John Fraser had been born in Kittwhistle, Inverness-shire and was a bootmaker, shown in the 1851 Census as living in High Street, Wick, Caithness, Scotland. Her mother, Jean Grant, had been born in Wick. Jean's father, the local stonemason, had helped to build the Old Parish Church and that is where Jean had married John. Jean made extra money for the family by both making clothes for her own family and also dresses that she sold to the community. Previously all hand sewn, John had purchased her the recently invented sewing machine. This new technology had been patented by Isaac Singer who had begun large scale manufacturing.

As a child, Christina attended a Free Church school. In the Disruption of 1843, four hundred and fifty evangelical ministers had broken away from the Church of Scotland to form the Free Church. This had undermined the traditional parish schools and by 1847 the Free Church had five hundred and thirteen schools with central funding for over forty-four thousand children taught in them. Previously, the Church of Scotland had provided basic education though most of the students in Christina's school were boys. Christina also attended a Dame School that had been informally set up by a spinster to teach girls reading, sewing and cooking. For most girls this was their only access to education outside home schooling by parents.

Christina would eventually gain access to a college and as these institutions had no entrance examination, students could choose which lectures to attend but after two years most students left without a specific qualification. Christina and other women were only allowed to gain a Lady Literate in Arts qualification. It was popular with women because it could be studied externally through correspondence.

As a child, with her siblings, her favourite place to play was the Castle of Old Wick, known by some as The Old Man of Wick, built in the twelfth century when the region was part of the Norwegian Earldom of Orkney. The castle was thought to have been built by Earl Harald Maddadson in the 1100s. The major remnant of the castle was a tall tower sitting on the very edge of the cliff, about half a mile south of the bay. There were also the remains of a four storey building that held a dramatic position on a spine of rock, projecting into the North Sea, between two deep, narrow gullies. The children would play heroes and heroines, fighting on each side of the deep cut rock-ditch, a previous moat once spanned by a drawbridge. Christina's brothers had homemade bows and arrows that they fired through the narrow window slits. Her father had an intense interest in Scottish history and had guided them through the building several times, pointing out the original barracks, the brewery and the chapel. The castle in 1644 had come into the control of the Sinclair family and Christina's father John, felt a hereditary bond. This was through his wife Jean Grant, daughter of Barbara Sinclair with her lineage going back to William 1st Earl of Caithness, the last Earl (Jarl) of Orkney, a Norwegian and Scottish nobleman and builder of the Rosslyn Chapel, in Midlothian. The family line had also been documented back to Freskin, a Flemish nobleman who settled in Scotland during the reign of King David I. Freskin becoming the progenitor of the Murray and Sutherland families. It was believed he belonged to a large group of Flemish settlers who came to Scotland in the mid-twelfth century.

Another local castle, three miles north of Wick, was the fifteenth century Castle Girnigoe. It was here that one of Christina's ancestors, David Sinclair had been imprisoned by his brother George, the 4th Earl of Caithness. This had happened during the reign of

Mary, Queen of Scots. Mary had been having dinner at the Palace of Holyrood, with her private secretary, David Rizzio, when her husband Lord Darney and a group of Protestants broke in and killed Rizzio, claiming he was having an affair with Mary. Mary escaped to Dunbar Castle in East Lothian where she was joined by friends including George Sinclair, Earl of Caithness. After the Battle of Torran-Roy, George Sinclair eventually defeated the Earl of Sutherland and the Murray Clan. George imprisoned his own son, John Sinclair, in Girnigoe Castle, charging him with rebellion. He was held for seven years, after which his father fed him a diet of salted beef and nothing to drink. John died, insane from thirst. David Sinclair, George's younger brother had also supported the Murrays and was imprisoned but gained release.

On longer summer days Christina's family would attach their horse to the family dray and travel along the bumpy coastal track to the imposing ruins that clung to the rocky cliffs at the southeast end of Sinclair's Bay, near Noss Head. The site was actually the ruins of two castles, a fifteenth century castle built by William Sinclair, 2nd Earl of Caithness, and the later remains of the Castle Sinclair.

Christina's ancestors had become landowners in the Caithness area when David Sinclair married Marie Calder. Due to the marriage the lands of Dun, Forss and Baillie, were granted to the Sinclair's by the Earl of Caithness. It was given to the family with the right of succession to David's sons William, Alexander and Henry.

One lasting side effect of this heritage was the insistence of Christina's grandmother, Barbara Sinclair, that Christina be taught French. Christina's mother Jean had learnt and in turn instructed Christina. There were practical reasons, as many of the traders and fishermen who came across the English Channel to Wick from Normandy used French. However, for the Fraser women, especially Barbara, it had more to do with social status. Norman French had historically been used in Scotland and the early Scoto-Norman families preferred the French culture to native Scottish culture. French was the language of the land-owning classes, Gaelic the language of the peasants.

Of the peoples of Scotland, the Caithnessians were considered well made. They had developed the best of the amalgamation of the two original races, Celtic and Scandinavian. The men were thought hardy and active, the women generally exceedingly good-looking. Outsiders found them to be shrewd, practical and good at business. In the case of Christina, she had been favoured with all these features.

John, like Jean, also had a strong clan connection to this area. Though the Frasers had predominantly lived in the Inverness region, Highland blood coursed through his veins. John's father, also John, was born

1760 in North Uist in the Outer Hebrides. His father Donald had been a share farmer on the island of North Uist, the son of a soldier. John's great grandfather, also John, had been in the Green Howards (Alexandra, Princess of Wales Own Yorkshire Regiment). He had fought in the seven-year Austrian War of Succession, being wounded in the Battle of Fontenoy in 1745. This had resulted in him being given a grant of land.

Family documentation traced his heritage to Hugh Fraser, 1st Lord Lovat, chief of the Clan Fraser of Lovat, a clan in the Scottish Highlands and strongly associated with Inverness where the Fraser clan gained lands in the thirteenth century. On special occasions, John proudly wore his family crest, a buck's head with the motto "Je suis prest", "I am ready". He could remember his father taking the family to see the clan seat, Beaufort Castle or Castle Dounie situated on the right bank of the river Beauly thirteen miles west of Inverness.

Christina's family enjoyed their coastal rambles and the wide selection of wildlife along the way. There were many species of seabirds, but Christina's favourite was the puffins. These loud but placid birds lived in large colonies on the coastal cliffs, either nesting in crevices among the rocks or in burrows in the soil. The birds seemed curious about humans, and their cute waddling was often mimicked by the children. Her brother John would copy the pig-like grunts and growing noises that came from the colony.

Christina was always amazed at the grace of the sea birds, generally harmless but during May and June, the children had to be vigilant of the Great Skuas. This seabird spend most of the year at sea but they behave violently when their breeding area is intruded and they could become dangerous, banging their beak on the head of the intruder. As with most things, her brother John had learnt this the hard way with one gashing his eyelid causing it to bleed.

Christina had always been fascinated by the giant stacks, standing like centurions guarding the coast. Some of them had been hollowed with arches, waves surging through, shooting up pillars of foam. One in particular was John's favourite. Just south of Wick at Hempriggs, two huge pillars had formed, conical rocks so perfect they looked artificial. The passage between the rocks so wide a boat could pass between.

Though time rarely permitted her father to take long breaks from his work, John felt it important to lose a day's work now and then for family time. Weekdays were busy and church meetings meant Sundays were also filled with gatherings, prayer services and outreach work. For their Saturday afternoon outings, Jean would pack her strong wicker basket, with its tartan lining, with family favourites. There would be a loaf of fresh bread with butter and baked meats, fish and potato balls and pasties that were wrapped in linen cloth to keep them fresher, and there was always a homemade fruit pie. John would gather water from a local stream with Jean adding the lemon and sugar she had brought with her to make lemonade. Because Jean and John both had Sinclair heritage, a large piece of Sinclair tartan cloth was used as a blanket to sit on and enjoy the peace away from the ever increasing town noise. John would read to the children from one of the two newspapers that were available in Wick, the *John O'Groats Journal* had been established in 1836 and the *Northern Ensign* in 1850, both of which John thought expounded Liberal views on politics. After lunch, the family would play games, the girls preferred jacks but John preferred marbles. Jean would insist that they all participated in Drop the Handkerchief, Blind Man's Bluff or Statues. Once home, in the evening the family would gather in the parlour and the children played cards. Jean and John were appalled at gambling but saw cards as an enjoyable way of helping the children learn about mathematics, and specialist cards helped with geography, history and science. The geography cards had been developed by John Wallis in 1803, having descriptions that included national dress, capital city, longitude and latitude, religions and universities. One such card was about Caffraria, where a clue included: 'The huts of the Caffrees are strong and compact, covered with a mixture of earth, clay and cow-dung. The doorway is so low that they must crawl on hands and knees to enter. The men show great courage in attacking lions or any beast of prey.'

When the time permitted a longer excursion would be taken to Whaligoe Haven, a small inlet surrounded on three sides by two hundred and fifty foot cliffs. The term "goe" meant "rocky inlet" and the children had been told by their grandfather that Whaligoe had been named because of a dead whale that had washed up there. Located seven miles south of Wick it was used by a few fishermen as their base. On the cliff stood a row of stone fishermen's cottages and a cooperage used during the herring season to make the barrels needed to store the salted herring. The inlet could be accessed by approximately three hundred and thirty flagstone steps in a series of zigzags with five hairpin turns, descending the steep slopes with only a low stone wall on the seaward side for protection. The sea mist often resulted in the stones being wet and slippery, so the children had to descend slowly and carefully to avoid injury. In 1793, a Captain David Brodie had paid a local stonemason to make a new set of stairs, replacing the rough original path, making it easier to access the inlet. John and Jean would normally stay at the top entrusting John Junior with the supervision. Christina found the descent to be both fun and beautiful. Wildflowers adorned the surrounds and seabirds swooped and screeched as if attempting to deter these unwelcome visitors. In 1786, when Thomas Telford had been hired to survey the coast of Caithness in search of good harbours for the herring fleet, he had described Whaligoe as a 'dreadful place,' open to huge swirling waves driven by northern storms. As a harbour it would have been very unsuitable but at the bottom of the step was a flat grassy area called the Bink. This contained at one end a small building to store salt used in curing fish. At the other end were more steps leading to a rocky shelf called the Neist. John had explained that ships using the inlet as a haven would moor against the rocks on the north side as it was the most sheltered. Small fishing boats would be pulled out of the water and stored on the Neist. There was also a winch that would have been used to haul the boats ashore. The family never visited in the summer herring season when twenty or more fishing boats would be in full production. The children found the ascent back up the steps a hard slog and Christina imagined how difficult it would have been carrying baskets laden with fish to the top so they could be taken to Wick for sale.

On warm sunny days, the children would set out for walks over the open moorlands. Vegetation here, low growing in the acidic soils, mainly consisted of heaths, sedges, rushes and hardy grasses. The heath covered fields often offered the opportunity to pick wildflowers such as bell heather, harebell or Scottish blue bells, Scottish thistle and bog myrtle. Care had to be taken to avoid the swampier areas and the clouds of biting mi-jee (midges) that lived there and laid their eggs in the wet soil. Christina would crush the leaves of the bog myrtle and rub it on her skin, as not only did it have a pleasant citrus smell but also acted as a natural repellent for midges. Not all plants were welcoming, the sundews, butterwort and bladderworts were all carnivorous, luring, capturing and digesting insects that gave them a rather unpleasant stench. Plants were not the only dangerous moorland inhabitant. The area also contained adders that grew up to seventy-five centimetres in length and had a dark zigzag pattern down their backs. Though venomous, they were timid creatures preferring to avoid human contact. Christina had seen a few, mostly in the afternoon when they were most active. She didn't know anyone who had been bitten but local dogs seemed the most common victim.

One such walk took them up the Hill o' Many Stanes, dominated by around twenty-two rows of Bronze Age stones arranged in a fan shape along the hillside. Barbara, their grandmother, had told them never to touch the stones as this was a burial site and she had heard of a farmer who took one of the stones home to build the kiln. The stone had burst into flames, terrifying the man, who immediately took it back and never touched them again.

There were places from which Christina and her siblings were banned, especially an area called the

Tinkers Cave. The tribe of mainly dark-skinned gypsies, living in some of the caves, were folk that had been involved in the tin trade. Men, women and children, some naked, lying on straw grass and bracken spread over the rock, driftwood and peat fires for warmth and cooking. Stones were used as tables and chairs.

Their dogs, which were numerous and vicious, acting as guards and protectors. Broken noses and scars were a common disfigurement. Tinkers were considered a scourge in the local towns. There were several tribes, the MacFees, the Newlands, the Johnstones and the Williams and although they called themselves tinsmiths, Christina's father considered them all beggars and thieves. She had noticed that a common feature was their use of English rather than the local Gaelic, but they spoke with a whining tone.

In the fishing season another group added to the perceived threat to locals. Hawkers wandered the streets with their baskets attempting to sell anything and everything. Coming from the south, John also saw them as an enormous evil, expert thieves and beggars.

In saying that, John felt sympathetic towards others who had arrived. Toward the end of the eighteenth century, tenant farmers had been evicted from their homes across the Scottish Highlands to make way for sheep farming. From 1792 onwards, displaced families began to arrive in places like

Badbea, a small area of rough, steeply sloping land, south of Wick, squeezed between the high drystone walls of the sheep enclosures and the precipitous cliffs above the North Sea. When the families arrived they were given small plots to farm, but had to clear the land, hack out the plots from the steep slopes, and build their own houses from the stones they found. He knew the area, exposed terrain open to North Sea gales. He wondered how true the rumours were about children and sheep having to be tethered to prevent them being blown off the cliffs and into the sea.

The smells of Christina's childhood were dominated by the strong rotten egg smell of cured herring. During the curing, just enough salt is used to prevent the raw herring from rotting while allowing it to ferment. Christina had heard one customer arriving to purchase new heels for his boots, describing the herring as being similar to a corpse that had been decomposing in a bog for several week. But the reality of life had become the over one thousand fishing vessels that were based at Wick for the summer season. Some men lived on their boats, others in dormitories above the curing sheds. Many men trekked for hundreds of miles across wild country for a chance of work for pay. There were also "herring lassies" spending twelve weeks each summer gutting and packing the herring then at the end of the season moving south to Great Yarmouth and Lowestoft for work in the mills.

The herring, once packed into barrels, was exported by boat to England, Scandinavia, Russia and the U.S. The town also had over six hundred coopers making the large number of barrels needed from local oak.

Pulteneytown was another place where Christina was not allowed to venture alone. Built as a new herring fishing town it had an abnormal number of transient men wandering the laneways. It had been built in order to supply work to the Gaels evicted during the 1750 to 1860 Highland Clearances. Like Badbea, this had resulted from wealthy, often foreign landowners enclosing their fields, forcing famers to move into crofting communities working in the fishing, quarrying and kelp industries. After 1815, these communities became overcrowded, thus the landowners often paid the fares of many to immigrate to new lands such as America, Canada, Australia and New Zealand. The new harbour at Pulteneytown was constructed at a cost of forty thousand pounds, but from the beginning struggled as the easterly gales lashed the ships seeking anchorage.

Christina was the fourth of six children, Barbara, John, Mary, Jean and Rebecca. In many ways the children led a sheltered life. Generally, Wick was God-fearing, with the Sabbath strictly observed and prayer meeting strongly attended. John and his wife were members of the community's strong temperance movement, driven to a large extent by local women who suffered as a result of their husband's wages being squandered on alcohol, especially cheap local whisky.

# Chapter 5

Since the 1840s John had been a strong spokesman for the Total Abstinence Society, calling for the abolition of all intoxicating drinks. He was concerned that for Scots, like the Irish, it was the ordinary people that drank a great deal of whisky. He had heard that in Glasgow, there was one liquor outlet for every one hundred and fifty people, supplemented by the illegal "shebeens" that served up a mix of whisky and methylated spirits. This consumption of whisky had played a central role in Scotland's heritage, the term whisky derived from the Gaelic "uisage-beatha", meaning "water of life".

John had adopted the beliefs of Primitive Methodism which had differed from other Wesleyan Methodists in that it allowed and encouraged preaching and services in the open air, in public parks or community halls. As an independent church it had less restrictions and traditional allegiances. He also felt that as they allowed women as leaders within the church, including as preachers, the Primitive Methodists were far more welcoming and inclusive.

Because of this open and encouraging religious affiliation he felt comfortable standing in the public square of Wick spreading the word of the evils of drink and the ruination of people's lives. He was particularly concerned that many employers paid their workers in cheap whisky rather than money. This also affected local businesses like his own, as this meant these families had less money to purchase his product, in his case, shoes. With other members of the Wick Chamber of Commerce, they wrote to the Duke of Sutherland with their concerns. He had lent his support, indicating that he would ensure all fishermen who worked for him would be paid in money. The chamber and its members' actions were, however, causing concern among some elements of the rural community as their livelihood relied on making and selling their locally distilled whisky.

One later surprising supporter, considering his connection with the opium trade, was James Matheson, member of parliament for Ross. At a temperance meeting, he declared his intention not to employ anyone 'found guilty of intemperance.' These types of announcements also added to those who opposed people like John Fraser. It was part of their very culture and nature to consume whisky, many resented anyone trying to stop them. While giving public addresses, John had been spat on and had rotten fruit and fish guts thrown at him. Though unpleasant, he had never considered them a direct threat aimed specifically at him, just his message.

John wrote articles for the *Northern Abstinence Advocate*, a monthly periodical, first published in Wick in 1840. Though the bulk of publications, pamphlets and books were published and distributed from the central organisations, such as the Scottish Temperance League based in Glasgow, John's local society funded the *Advocate*. Besides calling for sobriety, John's articles encouraged people to meet and form their own local societies. He had to call himself a "teetotaller", a temperance activist totally opposed to alcohol. He was also a Christian but in his own mind he separated the goals. He wasn't out to convert men's souls, which was the preacher's job, he just wanted to change their lifestyles and thus reduce the negative behaviour he saw in the streets of his community that was resulting from the excesses of drink. Though he had friends who considered consumption of mead, cider and wine a less serious problem than the consumption of locally distilled whisky, John saw the evil in all alcohol. He would often quote Proverbs 23:31-35 from his King James Bible.

"Look thou upon the wine when it is red — at the last it bites like a serpent, and stings like a viper. Your eyes will see strange things, and your heart will utter perverse things. They have stricken me, I was not sick

— they have beaten me, but I did not feel it. When shall I awake, that I may seek another drink?"

John knew that the Church of Scotland did not support the temperance movement as they were concerned the movement was led by laymen and secessionist churchmen. As such, they were seen as a threat to the established church, who saw themselves as the guardians of spiritual and moral health of the nation. It wouldn't be till 1848 that the Church of Scotland would appoint its own committee to enquire into intemperance. This was despite the church's own concerns about the fact that alcohol could be bought on a Sunday, the Sabbath, and the drunken hangovers from a Saturday's overindulgence was being blamed for increasing church absenteeism.

After all, the use of wine in the holy sacrament was considered a pillar of the church. John laughed when he considered the fondness of alcohol and inebriety levels of some ministers he had met. He knew that whisky was almost venerated as part of the custom of births, marriages and funeral. John thought of a recent wedding he attended where the parson was also a great cattle dealer at the market, the leading dancer at the wedding, the toastmaster and one of the last to slide off his chair at the drinking bout.

John would speak to other businesspeople of Wick and surrounding communities to garner support. He was a supporter of the Gothenburg system, where business owners would be paid incentives to sell food and soft drinks with some of the profits being put back into community projects, such as libraries. In 1841, a like-minded businessman, Anthony Doull, agreed to have his hotel, the John O'Groats Tavern, change to an "alternative and respectable refreshment venue", which was dry but sold a range of non-alcoholic drinks and served food. Both were pleased when the change was a success, but John could see it was doing little to change general community habits as the hotel attracted and met the requirements of already "respectable" clientele who could afford these services.

John financially supported the building of Wick Temperance Hall in 1842 that could accommodate a thousand dried-out souls. He believed in putting back into his community that had always supported him. He also realised that a movement, no matter how important, needed a base. A visual reminder of its ongoing significance, a rallying point.

Juvenile temperance societies had also been set up in the 1850s and were active in the community attracting a considerable number of members. Though trying to attract people from all classes, it was mainly youth from the middle class, churchgoing families who attended regularly. John Junior and others like him making up the organising team. These juvenile societies were also closely linked to the local churches Sabbath Schools.

The three eldest Fraser children also helped their parents with the Band of Hope movement. These were gatherings of young people to encourage them to adopt a sober lifestyle. To motivate children to join and remain members, the group held outings, offered music lessons, helped with basic literacy skills, established orchestras and produced their own magazine. Meetings began with a temperance hymn, a prayer, followed by a speech from a fellow member. The meetings usually concluded with musical items or recitations. Once a year, the community held a Band of Hope Gala Day with John very active in the organising committee. Jean, Barbara, Mary and Christina would help the ladies committee with painting signs, posters and organising the food and games for the day. John Junior would walk around town handing out pamphlets about the day. The day aimed to attract young recruits with the pleasurable elements of music, games, food and water. Christina, like her grandmother, was good at drawing and enjoyed helping to design the pamphlets and paint banners with the mottoes "Happy Home" and "Stand Fast".

Christina also helped at the Wick Fishermen's Coffee House and the Wick Mechanics Institute. These places offered, mostly men, places to relax, read and be educated, that were alcohol free. The venues provided newspapers, magazines, local notices, leaflets and books. Being as fluent in Gaelic as English, Christina would read to the men or help with writing letters. Sadly, her clients were few, many just wanting a dry, comfortable and warm place out of the cold winds or icy rain.

Conflict between the temperance community and especially the fishing community came to a head in 1853 once the Conservative MP, Forbes Mackenzie, introduced the Public Houses (Scotland) Bill. This forced the closure of pubs in Scotland at ten p.m. on weekdays and on Sundays. Resentment ran high with temperance leaders threatened and property damaged. To Christina and the other Fraser children this conflict had mainly taken the form of men calling out at meetings or the occasional name calling, some jibes actually educated, like the biblical, Rechabites, or the Greek Nephalists, but most comments took the form of foul gutter terms.

This all changed one cool spring evening when John Junior was sent by his father, to walk his sister Christina home. She was only thirteen and had been helping set up for a meeting of the Band of Hope in the Temperance Hall. After walking along Louisburgh Street and Shore Lane they turned the corner towards the river and their home in High Street. Huddled in the shadows was a gang of four youths, notable for their stench of rotten fish and whisky. John Junior instinctively stepped in front of Christina but was pushed to the ground. As he attempted to stand, one of the youths hit him over the head with a cosh, a bag of some type, filled with sand. While he was down, two of the youths kicked him several times then pulled off the boots his father had made him. The four spoke a coarse Highland form of Gaelic but Christina could understand most of what they said. The other two turned their attention to her. She could smell the decay of their foul black teeth and as one grabbed for her cloth drawstring bag, she felt his dirty claw-like nails ripping at her sleeve. She knew she should just give it to him, but it was special to her. Though it only contained some paper, a pencil, handkerchief and small purse with a few coins, her mother had made it. The fabric of red, forest green and navy was that of the Grant family tartan. It was made from the remnants of an old family kilt and her mother had sewn a pattern of Scottish thistle on the base. Christina felt the sleeve of her dress detach as the youth ripped off her cashmere shawl. She heard them yell to John that this was for their father trying to stop the whisky. The four ran off in the direction of Wick Harbour taking John's shoes and Christina's purse and shawl. They laughed and yelled abuse as they headed down the hill, throwing Christina's bonnet back and forth.

This was not the first threat the family had faced. John's wife had been sworn at by a passer-by while standing out the front of their house and two weeks earlier a large cobble stone had been thrown smashing the glass in John's workshop window.

John and Jean had been talking about a move to Edinburgh for several months, but it was originally driven by the thought of proving better educational and employment opportunities for their children. This had now changed to fear. John realised the stance he had taken and his high profile he and his family had in the Wick community had become a threat to both himself and his children. The decision was made, the family commenced packing their trunks for the move.

# Chapter 6

Gaining passage from Wick to Edinburgh's port of Leith was both easy and relatively inexpensive. Many ships arrived during the herring season laden with hopeful seasonal workers and businesspeople. Most captains were eager to have return paying passengers thus fares quoted were negotiable.

They boarded a steamer, *City of Aberdeen,* belonging to the Aberdeen, Leith & Clyde Shipping Company. This was a wooden paddle ship that had been built in 1835.

They all stood on the deck as they watched their home slowly disappear. Their once tiny community now had nearly seven thousand residents, it boasted forty-six grocers, seven bakers, twenty tailors and thirteen dressmakers. The shoreline's once rugged rocks and small beaches were crammed with countless herring boats, the clear crisp Highland air now marred by chimneys belching out black smoke.

Fortunately, the seas were calm as they steamed down the east coast of Scotland through the North Sea then into the Firth of Forth, part of the river's drainage basin. They passed the Martello tower, a small defensive fort built 1809 at the time of the Napoleonic Wars to defend the entrance of Leith Harbour. They finally arrived at Victoria Dock in Leith on the north bank of the river, The Water of Leith.

After disembarking, John and his family boarded a train at North Leith Station on Commercial Street, Leith, which would take them to Canal Street Station in Edinburgh's Old Town. The Edinburgh, Leith and Newhaven Railway Company had been formed in 1836 to connect the city of Edinburgh with the harbours on the Firth of Forth. It had developed following an Act of Parliament, but construction was difficult, requiring the digging of a long tunnel which opened in 1847. The tunnel was on a steep incline and was worked by rope haulage. Their destination, Canal Street, was a short dray ride from their new home where John planned to set up his shoemaking business.

For Christina and her siblings this was all new and exciting. It was their first time out of the royal burgh of Caithness, their first ocean voyage, first time to a large city and now riding in this amazing new technology. The tunnel was the most amazing part. At a length of one thousand and fifty-two yards (nine hundred and sixty-two meters) it was lit by gas lights and operated by a stationary engine and endless cable. A steam driven locomotive had hauled the carriages in open air sections from the port, and horses were still used to pull carriages into the station. Not that the children noticed but the station was very cramped, with two very short platforms.

# Chapter 7

In the census of 1861, the family was living at 9 Greenside Place, Edinburgh. Christina's brother John had gained employment as a lithograph printer and Jean a shoe binder. The area where they lived was at the top of a carriageway called Leith Walk. Many of the inhabitants had workshops and forges, some timber yards, marble workshops, foundries, flint and glassworks. With its old, cobbled stone streets, built on the grounds which belonged to the Carmelites or "White Friars", it was three hundred and fifty feet above sea level and offered views down to the Forth and beyond. A densely populated residential area, with narrow dark alleys and high tenements, up to nine storeys. The area consisted of the northwest ridge of Calton Hill.

John had communicated with preachers from the Primitive Methodist Church in Edinburgh who had recommended him setting up his business in the New Town that had been built in stages between 1767 and 1850. The first stage of new suburbs had followed the natural contours of the land with a principal thoroughfare along the ridge. The initial major streets named George, after the king at the time, George III, Queen Street, and St Giles Street, after the city's patron saint. The latter was rejected as St Giles was the patron saint of lepers and was also the name of a slum area on the edge of London. Therefore, the street was called Prince Street after the king's eldest son the Prince of Wales.

The Second New Town development occurred between 1800 and 1830. Townhouses and larger houses with back lane entrances for stables generally occupied the east-west streets, with blocks of flats and tenements, along north-south streets. Shops were restricted to the lower floors of the north-south tenements.

The third new town where John would locate his family was developed on the slopes of Calton Hill. It was built after the Regent Bridge was constructed over a deep ravine called Low Calton that was occupied by old and ill built streets. It separated Calton Hill from the Old Town.

The family's new home was a four-storey stone building with John's boot making business on the ground level. A short distance up Leith Walk stood St Mary's Catholic Cathedral.

Once settled in Edinburgh, Christina was enrolled in the Edinburgh Institute for Young Ladies at 37 George Square. The school had adopted the new concept of a central location, a building offering a range of disciplines including science which was becoming a major focus. It offered reading rooms where girls could study under the careful supervision of a lady superintendent. Prior to this, girls "took classes" which involved moving from house to house where different lessons would be offered. Though providing content it was fragmented, time wasting and lacked planned intellectual development.

The school Christina attended charged fifteen Guineas a year, a high price but John recognised Christina's potential and was happy to pay. Christina's older sisters Barbara and Mary had both attended Dame Schools where they had been taught basic reading, writing, simple commercial calculations, needlework and the art of cooking. Their mother Jean eventually took over their education through home schooling and the girls had finished their formal education prior to moving to Edinburgh. Younger sister Jean struggled at school so became her father's assistant in the shoe making business.

These were happy times in this new life. For the first time the children were allowed to celebrate Hogmanay. This was the Scots word for the last day of the old year and synonymous with the celebration of the New Year. For some reason, the community in Wick had suppressed the celebration due to its link with the consumption of alcohol. Fireworks exploded in the city of Edinburgh, Christina and her siblings were given a new day present of fresh fruit. The family also celebrated the tradition of ciad-chuairt, or first-foot. John had organised for one of the local preachers to come early in the morning to be the "first-foot" to enter their new home. This tradition was based on the belief that the first person who entered the home on New Year's Day, is seen as bringing good fortune for the coming year. Christina had attended the watchnight service with her family. A late-night service held on New Year's Eve, the seventh day of Christmas. She particularly enjoyed this service as it was a night of singing and praying, a happy family time. She loved the singing, especially the joyous *Auld Lang Syne*. The text had been written by Scottish poet Robert Burns in 1788 but was based on an old Scottish folk song.

# Chapter 8

In 1861, aged nineteen, Christina applied for the position as governess for the Ross family at 3 Lisburn Terrace, Bishopwearmouth, Sunderland, England. Her father was uncertain of this, as becoming a governess, hired to impart ladylike qualities to her charges, would be seen by many as forfeiting her own status as a lady. However, at the time, becoming a governess was the only means of earning a living for women of gentle birth or background. Christina's father had been reassured, as it had been a preacher at their church gathering who mentioned he had been contacted by a gentleman whose wife was unwell and was looking for a governess. The family, though in England, were of Scottish origins, the mother preferring to use her native Gaelic. The father wanted his children taught their lessons in English but also be taught to speak Gaelic. The Ross family also had a pianoforte and wanted the governess to be able to teach the children music. Though not particularly accomplished in this area Christina knew the basics, enough to teach young children.

To take up the position she had caught a train from Edinburgh crossing the English border at Berwick-upon-Tweed then down the east coast to Newcastle. It is here she met for the first time Joseph Ross, her new employer. The twenty-six-year-old glass maker was tall and muscular, a glow of redness in his thick hair with large hands of a person engaged in physical labour. He was well spoken and dressed in a single-breasted jacket extending to mid-thigh. He wore a waistcoat, his trousers were cut from a narrow check cloth, and he looked uncomfortable in his high, starched collar and necktie. He led her to a horse drawn hansom cab for the ten-mile ride to Sunderland.

Joseph talked about his town and seemed proud of its development. As they crossed the River Wear, he pointed out the iron bridge that had been built in 1796 and commented that it was the second cast iron bridge built in England and at one time the biggest single-span bridge in the world. Joseph described it as, 'a triumph of new metallurgy and engineering ingenuity.' Joseph explained that the locals used to rely on a ferry to cross the river and that the bridge design had become popular as the pattern on local pottery. The hansom cab took them along High Street that Joseph called 'the lonnin.' They passed the Vaux Brewery, the Wearmouth Green and the church of St Michael and All Angels. Christina noticed the green was bordered by neat cottages and the almshouse, a hospital that dated back to 1727. As they passed Mowbray Park that had been opened in 1857, Joseph talked about the lord mayor, John Candlish, who was a noted glass bottle manufacturer in the town and also owned a glassworks in Seaham. Christina was impressed with the large houses with extensive semi-formal gardens and the elegant terrace houses.

The Ross's two storey stone home was located on the southern bank of the river Weir. On arrival she was introduced to Mrs Ramsay, the Ross's cook and house keeper. Christina quickly realised that the sour expression on her face matched an equally sour personality. A widow, she had worked for the Ross family and helped Mrs Ross to care for the children, the role Christina was about to take over.

'Your room is at the top of the back stairs on the left, I'm next door and don't like noise. We were coping very well without you, and stay out of my kitchen '

Looking out her attic bedroom window, Christina could see the spire of the St Michael's church. The room was small and sparsely furnished. There certainly was nothing particularly glamour's about her new role. The family she was to care for consisted of three children with a mother who was unwell. Agnes was six, Elizabeth, four, and baby Joseph an infant. Agnes, who was attending school, was bright and outgoing, though initially resented this outsider who enforced rules that her mother was too ill to follow up on. Elizabeth was quiet and a few weeks after Christina's arrival complained of a sore throat, headaches and was experiencing fevers. Their father, Joseph, had sent for the doctor who immediately ordered her to be separated from the other children as she had swollen lymph glands on the front of her neck and was developing a rash. The doctor indicated he had seen several similar cases this week and believed it to be the onset of scarlet fever. Elizabeth suffered from vomiting and abdominal pain with red areas developing in her arm and elbow pits. Christina chose to remain in Elizabeth's room applying cool compresses in an attempt to lower her temperature, sadly the small frail girl died five days later.

Joseph admired the dedication that Christina had shown to the care of his daughter. She was selfless with her time and in reality, was putting her own health at risk. For five days she didn't leave Elizabeth's side, food being left by Mrs Ramsay at the bedroom door with fear of the disease spreading. Christina was shocked when after the funeral Mrs Ramsay took her hand squeezing it tightly.

'Thank you, miss, I'm sorry I misjudged you, please join me in the kitchen, I've made a cake.'

It was less than a year later that Joseph's wife Agnes died. She had been bedridden for much of the time that Christina had worked for them, thus Christina had taken on most of the responsibilities for running the family home, delegating duties to Mrs

Ramsay and entrusted to hire a new cleaning maid. She enjoyed her time with Agnes Junior and caring for infant Joseph, ensuring that Mrs Ramsay, now a supportive ally, was included in as many of the children's activities as possible. Christina sat as part of the family for meals, and it was no surprise that two months after Agnes's death Joseph travelled to Edinburgh with Christina where they were married. Their first child, a son, John Ross was born 1864, in Durham, a city in northeast England.

Joseph was not the type of man she had expected to marry. Christina had imagined she would end up with a person who was a free spirit, who enjoyed adventure. However these type of men seemed to be in very short supply. Perhaps they had all immigrated to the new worlds to make their fortunes or on mass had stereotyped governesses as a gaggle of prudes not worth the effort.

Joseph was a safe choice, he had good employment, was a church goer and proven family man. He respected her, though she was not really sure there was love and he had never mentioned the word. He was supportive, not passionate or even romantic, but she was sure his other qualities would be enough to make her happy. Her parents had been encouraging of the union and saw it as ensuring their daughters financial security.

Christina had not been with a man so had limited expectations of what being a wife meant. From their first night together their intimacy was brief and functional. Usually tired from a hard day of physical labour, Joseph would do his duty as a husband and be in a deep sleep minutes after his head hit the pillow. Some evenings Christina sought the shelter of the children's nursery as Josephs snoring was so loud. Except for the bed in which she slept with her husband, little changed from her time of being the family's governess. Previously he seemed to make more of an effort to talk to her, to tell her bits about his day, but there seemed less and less of these shared adult times.

# Chapter 9

Christina's husband Joseph Ross had been born in Sunderland, Durham in 1835. His father James Adam Ross was a farm labourer and his mother Elizabeth Laidler, a dairy maid. He had one brother, Thomas Smith Ross, born 1836.

Though they had never married James and Elizabeth's relationship had been one based on passion. Both families had disapproved as Elizabeth was only sixteen and James seventeen. James had also been in front of the local magistrate on several occasions charged with poaching. Though this had been dealt with as misdemeanours he had faced several lectures from the magistrate and on the third occasion spent a few weeks in prison. James always used the starving family plea but in reality was selling his game at a local inn, a fat pheasant fetching up to two shillings. He would argue with the magistrate that the land once was, and should be, free for the ordinary people like himself to hunt for rabbits or fish for food. However, to landowners, poaching was theft, pure and simple. The game on their estates was used not only for sporting ventures but provided food on the table and served as a "cash crop" when supplies were plentiful. Many landowner were also magistrates thus people like James were not likely to have a sympathetic ear listening to their cases.

One dark, stormy night as James was setting his traps for rabbits the estate's game keeper and three men caught him. Rather than risk him getting another light sentence they tied a rope around his neck and threatened to hang him. The men then beat him till he fell unconscious. The last thing he remembered was a warning that next time no one would find his body. Waking in the morning, he made his way to the dairy where Elizabeth tended to his cuts and as she did they made a pact to run away together, Elizabeth was already pregnant with Joseph.

The 1841 census showed Joseph aged six as an inmate at the Hensworth Workhouse, Jarrow, Durham. This was a small town on the banks of the River Tyne, eight kilometres west of Newcastle on Tyne. The British workhouse was a total institution, a place of education, work and residence for people unable to support themselves or their family. In Scotland they were usually known as poorhouses. For families like Joseph's, the introduction of new technology that replaced agricultural workers, and a series of bad harvests, meant by the 1830s the number of people needing poor relief was growing rapidly. The new Poor Law of 1834 attempted to resolve this by forcing people to enter workhouses to obtain support.

After 1835, many workhouses were constructed with a central building surrounded by work and exercise yards all enclosed by brick walls called "pauper bastilles". The buildings were seen more like prisons than institutions designed to help and support the poor. Humanely, the 1840s saw a separation of groups with children, no longer placed in wards with old, infirm, tramps and vagrants.

Each parish had a Poor Law Union that employed relieving officers, whose job it was to assess what relief, if any, they should be given. Joseph was allocated to a ward that held boys under fourteen years of age. After being stripped and checked over, his old clothes burnt, he was bathed and issued with a distinctive uniform, a striped cotton shirt, jacket and trousers, and a cap. Though a young age, Joseph still realised that certain uniforms meant different things. Pregnant single women had to wear red dresses while prostitutes were required to wear yellow dresses. On the day he entered the workhouse, two other boys were also admitted but both had to spend time in a "foul or itch" ward as they had scabies and were considered contagious.

Joseph found his ward consisted of a single large room with rows of cots with straw covering and a blanket. There was a bucket in the middle of the room used for sanitation. Despite this, the conditions in

Hensworth Workhouse were better than many. The food was based on a weekly ration and usually consisted of bread and gruel, a thinner version of oats and milk porridge, for breakfast, and for midday dinner some type of cooked meat and vegetables and supper bread and broth. Joseph found that he was at least fed every day, unlike when he was with his family, who often could not afford regular meals. Joseph considered himself fortunate as he had been told by a new arrival that while they were in Andover Workhouse, starving paupers were reduced to fighting over the bones they were supposed to be crushing for fertiliser just to suck out the marrow.

It was not till 1847 that the Consolidation General Order would be issued. This provided guidelines on issues such as diet, staff duties, dress, education, discipline, and redress of complaints.

The workhouses also provided education for children, but the people employed were untrained and poorly paid. Classes were large, full of unruly children, with little or no interest in learning. In 1845, legislation was passed that pauper children had to be able to at least read and sign their name.

Where possible, workhouses were linked with local industry. Parishes, through their Poor Law Unions, made up of local leaders, advertised for apprentice positions and were willing to pay any employer prepared to offer them. They saw this as a better long-term method of teaching skills and supporting apprentices and it was also cheaper than supporting them in workhouses. Children and their families often had no say in the matter, their employment organised without their knowledge or permission.

Joseph was fortunate as he had an uncle who worked as a labourer in a local glass-making factory, thus at the age of fourteen, he left the workhouse to take up an apprenticeship in the glassworks.

# Chapter 10

Joseph was an apprentice at James and John Hartley's Wear Glass Company, Monkwearmouth, Deptford, Durham, an English glass manufacturer established in 1836. The original owner, John, had retired in 1840 leaving his son James running the business. Wear Glass manufactured rolled plate glass with obscured ribbed finish, which was used in the roofs of railway termini. The company also made coloured glass, mainly used for church windows. Over seven hundred men worked at the factory. The men worked eight-hour shifts, which had recently changed from six hour in an attempted to become more efficient by reducing the number of changeover periods. The factory made a third of all sheet glass used in the country. Joseph found this initial apprenticeship useful in developing an understanding of the glassmaking process. He learnt about the quality and range of raw materials, the processes and infrastructure needed.

The Census of 1851 showed Joseph living with his uncle, Adam Laidler, a bottle house labourer, in Bottle Row, Durham. Joseph's mother Elizabeth was Adam's sister.

Joseph liked the work and showed a natural aptitude for glassmaking.

In 1853 he changed employment working for Walker, Fetherstone and Company. They owned the Wear Glass Bottle Company, also known as the Deptford Bottle Works. The factory made all kinds of bottles, and it is where Joseph honed his glassblowing skills. Here he was part of a team of five consisting of a "gatherer" of the molten glass, "blower" who shaped the bottle, "wetter off" who cooled the bottle, a "workman" and a "boy". The team were required to produce a specific number of bottles per shift. The team would be paid an additional rate for production above requirements. Joseph didn't like the process of the senior man being given the total payment and deciding how much each member of the team would receive.

Joseph mastered each of the steps. He learnt to gather the molten glass from the furnace on the end of a blowing iron. The glass was inflated by human breath to form a crude oval shape, a parison. It was then shaped by rolling it on a smooth stone table, the marver. Joseph would then reheat the parison in the furnace to allow it to be blown to the needed size. Pincers and other simple tools were used to help shape the bottle. Some bottles were left in a torpedo shape, others had the bottom pushed in to supply a stable base. He learnt to use "dip-mounds", a simple cylinder that did not open, instead the molten glass was blown to fill the tube then withdrawn vertically.

After mastering the basics at Wears, Joseph moved to Germany to improve his glassmaking skills. This travel at the end of an apprenticeship was common and called the journeyman years. The journeyman would keep a travel book and in each new town would get it stamped by officials both as a work experience record and residence registration. This documentation also protected the trade against imposters. Joseph went to work for Hans Siemens who had a glassworks in Dresden.

He worked as a journeyman, a name used by the trade guilds for skilled workers in a particular craft, employed by others, historically paid daily. Guilds ranked workers as apprentices, journeymen and masters. After Germany, he worked in factories in Yorkshire and Lancashire then travelled to North America working in New Jersey and Pittsburgh where he remained for about three years.

There were plenty of opportunities on offer, as from 1804 to 1860, nearly one third of America's glass was being made in New Jersey. Though dominated by a few large companies many small glassworks had also developed and Joseph gained employment with Whitall Brothers and Company in Millville, New Jersey with its headquarters in Philadelphia. The company produced bottles, jars and vials. After his time in America, Joseph travelled to

Canada working for short periods both in Montreal and Hamilton.

He returned to England and married Agnes Queen in Leith, Midlothian. Agnes had been born in Scotland and was six years older than Joseph. Agnes was a widow, her husband had been a publican who had married despite his family's objections. They considered Agnes pretentious, she refused to work with the family at the hotel, constantly wanted the latest fashions and insisting on the employment of a housekeeper/cook. Realising that if anything were to happen to him his family would disown her, he purchased a cottage in Agnes's name as protection. When he died, Agnes opted to take in boarders, one being a handsome and physically fit nineteen year old, Joseph. It was the mixture of infatuation with an older and more experienced woman and her flirtation that led to a sexual relationship, formalised by a private marriage ceremony. The couple had three children, Agnes, Elizabeth and Joseph Junior, though it was the housekeeper Mrs Ramsay who ran the house and family. Agnes was rarely at home, accepting any and all invitations from afternoon teas to evenings at the theatre or dining with friends. Joseph rarely attended, the excuse always related to his work obligations. By the time Agnes was pregnant with their third child they had separate rooms and Joseph could go weeks not seeing or talking to her. This all changed with the birth of Joseph Junior.

Complications resulted in Agnes becoming virtually bedbound, she suffered from hair loss and anaemia. Agnes opted to remain in her room, taking meals on a tray and refusing to see the children. Joseph realised the need to employ a governess as quickly as possible.

# Chapter 11

In the 1851 Census, Thomas, Joseph's brother, was working as a herd boy in Northumberland. He had lost contact with his brother but through relatives had a general understanding of what he was doing.

Thomas, like many of his generation from poor farm labour families, had a lack of opportunities but while working with other men on farms, he had learnt from them to read and write. Again, like many of his peers, he had heard the stories of the gold discoveries in the colonies and decided that he would apply as a farm labourer for assisted emigration. He left the farm, moving to Newcastle upon Tyne in search of any form of paid employment. Sunderland had become the most important shipbuilding centre in the country in the 1830s and by 1840, there were sixty-five shipyards. Over one hundred and fifty wooden vessels were built at Sunderland in 1850, when two thousand and twenty-five shipwrights worked in the town. In 1852, the first iron ships were built in Sunderland, and Thomas could see they were the way of the future. Though not planning on taking up this profession, he was pleased to get an apprenticeship as a shipwright. He worked for William Pickergill who in 1851 had set up a new shipyard in Southwick. The yard produced only wooden vessels for the coal trade. It was a tough job, the ships being built in the open air, in all weather conditions. Thomas had to learn all the practical steps in construction plus the basics of design.

As the apprenticeship was for seven years, it was 1858 before he completed his training and resumed his quest to emigrate to what he kept hearing was a land of greater opportunity.

Thomas had built his own wooden chest which held the tools of his trade. These included his adze, used for shaping and dressing wood, augers, for drilling holes in timer, beetle, a heavy iron mallet used to drive wedges into seams to open them so they could be sealed with oakum. He had slide rules for measuring, a pitch ladle used to pour boiling tar into deck seams to seal and make watertight. He used ochre, a red chalk to mark timbers and had a range of irons (jerry, horsing, reeming, and sail) each with a specific purpose.

Thomas arrived in Sydney 1858. He was a skilled assisted emigrant and gained work as a shipwright. His work consisted of repairing and building small craft. Though he remained as a journeyman, paid a wage but without a continuity of employment, work was plentiful. Being considered a respectable tradesman he found, like many of his colleagues, he had excess money which they invested in infrastructure development. Over time he set up his own small shipbuilding yard, repairing wooden ships and taking orders for new boats, from small skiffs to larger river craft. His boats were designed for harbour and river use thus tended to have shallow drafts. For Thomas, his trade and business assured access to social and financial success.

Shipping in the colonies was vital as water transport was so much easier than land. Shipbuilding had actually been banned until 1813, to prevent convicts from escaping. After that the trade flourished. Deep water sites along the bays and foreshore of Port Jackson attracted shipbuilders and soon schooners, cutters, ketches and ferries were built locally. The first Manly ferry was built in 1851 in the Thomas Chowne's Pyrmont yard. It was conveniently located next door to the Goodlet and Smith timber yard and Chowne built thirteen vessels over the next twenty years.

Thomas quickly realised that the shipbuilding community was very close, and in some ways, closed to outsiders. Most of the Master shipwrights and shipbuilders were Scots, Presbyterian, and all had arrived in the colony as free men. There were many fine hard-working men who were ex-convicts but to the free settlers they were still convict stock. The choice of a wife was thus a major consideration in terms of future professional and social connection.

Thomas married Ann Holland at St Andrew Scots Church. Ann was the daughter of a local master shipwright. They had two daughters, Elizabeth Jane (1861—1940) and Florence (1863—1926) both born in Balmain. For Thomas, the birth of a son was also considered important as the skills of shipwrights, at least in the colonies, tended to be handed down father to son.

Thomas had written to his brother Joseph about the amazing growth in the colonies and the opportunities for the establishment of new businesses. He encouraged him to emigrate.

He talked about the natural beauty of the land, its wealth of natural resources, the abundance of foreign investment in new industries and added about the quality of life. Thomas boasted to Joseph about the eighteen-foot sailing boat he had made himself and how the shipwright families held regattas, constantly improving their boat designs.

It took months for the letter to reach Joseph, then a further three months for the return reply.

Joseph, like Thomas, was ambitious. Though he was also a journeyman, but in the glass industry, the thought of establishing his own business appealed to him. He thought about his prospects in England but realised his limited capital and the size and skill base of his competition would make it impossible.

Joseph thanked Thomas for his consideration and began planning for the move to the other side of the world.

Christina was distressed that she only found out about Josephs plans when she discovered Mrs Ramsay sitting in her rocking chair by the kitchen fire, tears streaming down her aged face. Joseph had informed her that the family was moving and she would have to find another position. He had indicated that he knew of several people who would be happy to employ such a reliable and hard-working housekeeper. When Christina confronted Joseph about his announcement he was dismissive, indicating that had only made up his mind that day and had been going to tell that very evening, but she had been busy with the children.

The shock of it, the upheaval of her new safe world took its toll. She tried to suppress her anger but the more she did the greater depression she felt. It was akin to grieving, but when she wrote to her parents, her father's reply was blunt sighting acceptance and duty. At this she felt guilty. Joseph had provided the family with a good lifestyle, and saw this move as a great opportunity for a better life where he could be the master of his own destiny.

# Chapter 12

Joseph, Christina and children Agnes, Joseph Junior and baby John left Gravesend, England on 18th June, 1865 on the *Empress of the Seas*, chartered by the White Star Line. The ship was carrying four hundred and ninety-one passengers of which four hundred and seventy-five travelled steerage. Though they had sufficient money to pay for a second-class cabin, Christina insisted they save this for their new life. The decision was made to travel "tween decks" as assisted immigrants. Like themselves, many of the ships passengers were travelling on the free passage system conducted under the control of the Imperial Emigration Commissioners in England. This was designed to attract people with the skills that were needed in the colonies. In the Ross's case, Joseph's glassmaking skills.

The *Empress of the Seas* was bound for Rockhampton and during the journey Christina talked to these new acquaintances, discovering that a large number had actually paid their own way. They were travelling under a different scheme and had been enticed by the offers of farming land being supplied by the colonial government of Queensland as an inducement to emigrate.

When the colony of New South Wales was divided in December 1859 to form the northern colony of Queensland, the Queensland government immediately began a policy to populate the new colony.

With the encouragement of the Queensland colony's first governor, George Bowen, and premier, Robert Herbert, Queensland began direct immigration recruitment in London. This was highly competitive with the other Australian and British Empire colonies but from 1860 Queensland became the main Australian destination for assisted emigrants from the United Kingdom.

The Queensland colony had realised it could not afford the financial outlay of paying passage so opted for a self-funding scheme, offering land. This fitted with the colony's agrarian ideals of small freehold yeomen farms. Between 1861 and when Christina and her family arrived around fifty thousand British and Irish emigrants had made the move to Queensland.

The organisation of the policy, with selection and payment received, was done through an emigration commissioner and agent general, at 17 Gracechurch Street, London. The agent general in London was Henry Jordan who had been an English dentist and Wesleyan missionary before arriving in Brisbane in 1856. With the formation of the new colony, he had been elected to Queensland's first legislative assembly and was involved in the development of the 1860 Unoccupied Crown Lands Occupation Bill. This bill did not recognise any traditional ownership by the Aboriginal tribes and gave the government the right to sell or give land to emigrants. Land was Queensland's greatest asset, but rather than a specific title, each full paying adult emigrant received an eighteen pounds sterling warrant or voucher, which could be used to purchase land at one pound sterling per acre. To encourage families, a further eighteen pound sterling voucher could be claimed if the family had two children aged between four and twelve. After two years in the colony the family would be given a further twelve Pounds sterling voucher. For most emigrants this allowed the purchase of sixty-six acres. The land could be purchased anywhere in the colony to try and ensure that farms were viable.

# Chapter 13

Regardless of how each family had been attracted to take the ninety-six-day voyage, conditions could best be described as cramped. Because of the lack of space, the Ross family was only allowed one small canvas bag each for the items, including clothing and utensils they would need on the voyage. The rest was packed into trunks and stowed in the ship's hold. In bad conditions, many travellers were stuck in damp, dirty clothes and bedding for weeks. The shipping companies had supplied suggested requirements. For men it consisted of six shirts, three Guernsey or flannel, six pairs of stockings, one pair of stout shoes and one pair of stout boots, one suit and an extra pair of trousers, one light and one warm cap. For women, six chemises, six pairs of stockings, four petticoats, two of flannel and two light, two pairs of good shoes, one good coat with hood, one hat and one light bonnet. The colonial secretary was also concerned about the unpreparedness of many of the emigrants so also issued a similar list adding bedding including pillow, sheet and a pair of blankets, one water bottle, one wash basin, one plate, one pint drinking mug, one knife and fork, two spoons and three pounds of marine soap.

There was segregation on the ship, single men berthed in the bow, married couples and families in the middle and single women in the stern, closely supervised by a matron who was responsible for their physical and moral wellbeing. First class passengers had exclusive use of the poop deck and the saloon.

Steerage passengers were divided into messes of six to ten adults before boarding, and as a group, they drew their rations, cooked and ate. The groups in steerage had to do their own cooking with soups, oatmeal porridge, rice puddings and pies being the staples. The food was kept in the hold with pickled meat, mainly pork or beef in brine, flour, sugar and dried peas, kept in wooden barrels. After a few weeks Christina noticed that the grain and flour were infected with weevils, but no one complained.

Steerage passengers had berths which were wooden bunks that lined the wall and a long dining table in the middle. Each berth was designed for two people or in the case of the Ross family Christina, Joseph and John in an upper berth and Agnes and Joseph Junior below. As passengers were expected to bring with them their own bedding, Christina had sown together pieces of woollen cloth to give warmth and lined then with flannel for durability. She had made four of these, two for each bunk bed. The biggest problem with the bedding supplied was that it consisted of straw and attracted fleas and cockroaches. In fine weather people were allowed to bring their bedding onto the deck to shake it out and for airing. However, in storms and bad weather the bedding sometimes became damp or even soaked. Christina could remember during two storms the hatches breaking free resulting in waves of water crashing down into the steerage area soaking any standing or sleeping below. During the storms that lashed the Southern Ocean route, their ship tossed and rolled. At mealtimes it was a struggle to hold cups and plates on the table as they slid, often crashing to the floor.

The only ventilation "tween decks" was provided by hatches to the upper deck, which were locked tight during rough seas but still let a little water in during times of heavy wind driven rain. Regulations at the time required that ships had at least one toilet per hundred passengers but with regular outbreaks of diarrhoea these added to the hygiene concerns. Vinegar and chloride of lime were used to wash the wooden floors which helped to prevent the spread of disease and made the ship smell better. Cloths were soaked in vinegar and hung on the back of the toilet door to be used by all. The toileting process became much worse in the storms, or during the night, when passengers in steerage were basically locked below deck with no light.

Each day was regulated with the emigrants having to be out of bed before seven a.m., with all the children washed and dressed before breakfast at eight a.m. The children had to attend the school classes provided by the shipping company, and it is here many learnt to read and write for the first time. Each mess group had to clean a certain area of the ship. Dinner was at one p.m., tea at six p.m., and lights out at eight p.m. Because of the danger of fire, the use of candles and lanterns below decks was restricted and in rough weather banned. The afternoon was free family time with Joseph and Christina allowed time on the main deck to enjoy the sun and sea air or for the children to play deck games when weather allowed, or reading, writing letters and diaries with many of the women taking the opportunity to mend and sew.

Though not complaining, Christina found the crowded environment foul. She was proud of herself as she did not suffer the seasickness that affected most of her fellow passengers including Joseph and Agnes. The odour of vomit was pervasive and mingled with the stink of unwashed bodies and cooking smells. Those who were not seasick often were sick just from the stench. Rainwater was collected but this had to be used for drinking, so sea water was used to bathe and clean. Christina was shocked at some of her fellow travellers' hygiene. There were both men and women who never washed and seemed to wear the same clothing every day.

On the brighter side, the ship had a passenger committee to help organise entertainment with dances and musical performances. Several people had fiddles and three squeezeboxes.

Religious services were offered and there was a weekly muster for inspection by the ship's surgeon (doctor). Each mess was also assigned a particular wash day with warm water from coppers.

The first land sighted was Madeira in July, then in August their ship rounded the Cape of Good Hope and Cape Agulhas in relatively calm conditions but they were tossed from one white cap to the next as the Roaring Forties blew them eastward across the Indian Ocean. Their first siting of land after leaving the African continent was in September at Cape Otway, the southern tip of the colony of Victoria. The ship then rounded the northern coast of Tasmania and passed Cape Howe, sailing up the eastern coast where conditions deteriorated with gales, rough seas and thick heavy rain. The next land sighting should have been Cape Morton but because of the conditions Captain Davies kept well out at sea heading for Keppel Bay. He knew the coast had a reputation for ships being driven onto rocky outlets or striking unmarked rocks.

Seven adults and a number of children had died on the voyage, mostly of diarrhoea, bronchitis and consumption. A total of eleven children were born during the voyage. Christina, as with all those on board, found these losses difficult to cope with. Regardless of age or gender their bodies being sewn into a piece of canvas or placed in a rough coffin, often knocked together by the ship's carpenter. Once weighed down with some pig iron, they were slipped down a plank into the sea, left to sink. Christina thought having the ensign flag draped over the bodies at least added a degree of dignity to the makeshift services.

The twin-screw steamship *Platypus* had steamed down the Fitzroy River to Keppel Bay to meet the *Empress of Seas*. By evening the process of transferring the emigrants and their luggage was complete. Thursday morning, the *Platypus* began the trip to the Rockhampton township and arrived at the Railway Wharf at five p.m. Joseph and his family, with the other emigrants, were taken to the Immigration Barracks. Here they were supplied with basic food but had to do their own cooking in a communal kitchen area. There were a series of warnings given, but the one that made Christina shudder was being instructed not to go too close to the banks of the Fitzroy River due to the crocodiles. Christina had seen drawings in books of these fearsome beasts, and eventually got to see one. It was dead and stuffed, displayed in the Commercial Hotel that stood in Little Quay Street.

Christina realised that here in the colony, spring was just beginning, but already the days were 28°C (83°F) and nights only dropped to 14°C (58°F). It was hot but muggy. Her long woollen dresses, crinolines, multiple petticoats and leather boots were totally unsuitable. Proprieties had to be observed, but the colony obviously had greater informality, the range of attire was far wider than home. Though clothing still seemed to denote and distinguish class difference, Christina noted that attempts had been made to adapt to the climate. People who had been in the colony for some time seemed to wear fewer layers, lighter fabrics and all had large, brimmed hats for sun protection. The servant girls, with tanned sleeveless arms, seem to prefer a simple top and sturdy skirt, some well above the ankle. There were Asians in loose fitting colourful clothing and others in loose peasant clothes with "coolie" hats. Pacific Island men bound for the sugar fields or mines looked strong and tough in just shorts and relative conformist greenish coloured shirts. Near the dock she had also noticed a group of men and women with very dark skin. She was shocked at the almost nonexistence of any clothing.

On the day trip to the immigration barracks Christina remembered seeing several general stores, one named Palmers, opposite the Bush Inn with a sign showing "Opened 1856", another, "Feez's" but it was in a tent. She saw the Rees & Jones wholesale merchants, Shaw and Capper a two storey imports and exports business and the offices of a newspaper, the *Bulletin*. There were other hotels, butchers, drapers, tailors, timber merchants, cabinetmakers and undertakers, boat and ship builders, blacksmiths and wheelwrights, iron mongers, saddlers and harness makers. There seemed to be everything that a person required. She noticed the hairdresser, tobacconist and shoemaker. There were also suppliers of non-essentials such as a watchmaker, jeweller, bookseller and dentist. There were even the signs of a social life in the form of the Cornstalk Hotel which offered a music hall. The dray driver told her that several of these had relocated after a big flood in the town in 1864.

'It's hard to believe now, looking at the river, but two people drowned in that flood, it was a beauty. Some locals called it a hurricane. Sheets of rain were being hurled by the gales coming in violent gusts, trees fallen like pins. Shaw and Coppers lost their iron roof as did the *Bulletin* offices. Marsden's Baths were completely flattened and the roof off the Otago boarding house just vanished. The worst hit were the dozens of tents below the creek, that lot had to run for their lives, saved by the customs house boat and taken to shelter in the gaol and church. There was this one fella, however, a Mr Featherstonehaugh, who tried to ride across. You should have seen him, fancy dresser complete with a white top hat. We were watching from Quay Street, and he dropped off his horse into the river, keeping downstream of his steed, buggered how one of the floating logs didn't get them both. Anyway, the current swept the pair downstream, but they made it, washed to the bank just below Belle Vue Hotel, bloody miracle, I reckon.'

Though the principal port and town in the Queensland colony, Christina soon realised why the locals called the town the 'City of the Three S', which were sin, sweat and sorrow. Located on a river, the region had rich grazing land and in 1859 gold had been discovered at Canoona. Miners had rushed to the town, but the gold field proved to be poor, thus thousands of would-be gold seekers were left stranded. By 1861, the town did have a newspaper the Northern Argus, bank and courthouse. Christina was pleased to see that a Primitive Methodist Church had opened in Fitzroy Street in January 1864. The town was also developing as the main port for the expanding Central Queensland hinterland, the main export being wool.

Because of the historic development, it was a male dominated community. Until the 1860s men outnumbered women two to one. After the 1860s this slowly changed but the arrivals were the wives and young daughters of emigrant families. The earliest settlers tended to be adventurous souls, prepared to rough it out, then conforming to the requirements of their adopted country. They had left their least liked traits and customs behind. For some it was as simple as taking off their coat and going out without it.

The town was based on a planned street grid. The east-west pattern featured alternating broad streets and narrow lanes. The lanes were called little streets such as Little Quay Street where the Ross's rented a small, partly-furnished cottage. Christina presumed that the town's founders had hoped that, like many English towns, there would be large homes built on the broad streets, with stable access at the back from the smaller lanes. She was certain that had only been a dream as most arrivals were poorer farmers and men of trade. On the few days of rain that occurred while the Ross's were in Rockhampton, roads and lanes turned to mud and slush. Christina had seen drays bogged and on East Street a bullock dray being unloaded as the animals could not pull its load out of a hole left by the recent removal of a tree stump. One day Christina was running home from the school when Agnes sank in the clay to her ankles. After much tugging the boot was left behind, given up as lost.

Christina developed a close friendship with the Primitive Methodist preacher Reverend John Hartley. From their first meeting a few days after they arrived in Rockhampton, Christina was amazed at his energy and faith. He was always cheery but expressed some concern about what he saw as his failure. Though he regularly visited the gold diggings, few souls were saved. In all weather, he put up with poor fare, hard beds and very little encouragement.

Rev. Hartley had endeared himself to the family and while Joseph was busy looking into the prospect of setting up a business, Christina would take the children to all his services. Agnes enjoyed spending time with other girls her own age, but Joseph Junior would sit sour-faced, brooding at being made to wear his best clothing and sit for hours. He hated wearing his knickerbockers, wide leg pants fastened below the knee, a matching vest and jacket. Most of the boys he met in this new land wore long trousers and light collarless shirts. Joseph felt like a baby.

Christina had enrolled both Agnes and Joseph Junior in the local school. The school had opened in 1862 and grown rapidly due to the emigration. The forty-five-foot long and twenty-foot wide timber building had divisions by age and catered for boys and girls. Christina had an interview with the headmaster, Mr Barfoot, and though Agnes looked forward to attending, Joseph Junior's body language and inattentiveness made it clear he was going to be a difficult student.

Christina's baby, John, had been unwell during the last part of the long ocean voyage. He seemed to be constantly distressed, high fevers, nights filled with crying. Christina considered herself fortunate as this colonial town had both a doctor and small hospital. Dr Callaghan had set up practice in

Rockhampton in 1861 after working in Melbourne, the capital of the Victorian colony. He had been appointed the district coroner, the government medical officer, and house surgeon at the hospital located near the riverbank on Victoria Parade. Dr Callaghan made time to visit John and had prescribed several medicines to try and reduce the fevers. Agnes would be sent to Mr Elias Rutherford who had set up his pharmacy, also in Little Quay Street, only a block from the Ross's cottage. Three times Rev. Hartley had been called to the Ross's rented cottage with John not expected to live till morning. Sadly, on the third occasion he died, aged eighteen months.

Joseph Senior had been disappointed with the size and scope of the town, thus had purchased a ticket on the first boat to Sydney. This had left Christina with their own baby, too sick to travel, and Joseph's two children. Christina felt very alone as John was buried in the local cemetery. It was not till after the graveside service that she could bring herself to walk to the corner of Quay and Denham Street where a small shop held the recently opened telegraph office. The message was dispatched to Joseph, care of his brother Thomas, in Sydney.

# Chapter 14

Joseph had sailed from Rockhampton only a few months after their arrival in Queensland. He travelled to Sydney, the capital of the New South Wales colony, as a steerage passenger on the *Boomerang*, an iron single-screw steamer with two masts owned by the Newcastle and Hunter River Steam Navigation Company. In October, Christina, who had seen to John's funeral and the repacking of their belongings, also travelled on the *Boomerang* but with a saloon class ticket.

To Joseph, sailing through the Sydney Heads to Port Jackson provided a combination of excitement and optimism framed by the beauty of a virtually untouched land. He noted that nearly all settlement appeared to be located on the southern shore, the north covered with lush green-grey trees which reached to the shoreline.

On the southern head of the harbours entrance stood a small lighthouse with keeper's residence. Besides being a fortification, Joseph could see someone raising flags which relayed news to the incoming ship. As the ship sailed further into the enormous harbour it passed a fort-like structure in the middle of the harbour and he noted the Martello Tower similar to the ones he had seen in England. The captain called the sandstone structure built on a jagged rocky outcrop, Fort Denison. Joseph could see the cannon placements and guessed it had been built to protect the colony from either foreign powers or pirate attacks. He wondered if it was related to threats of a European war with Russia which had escalated into the Crimean War. He also noticed the naval base on the southern shore that the captain called Garden Island. He could see three Royal Navy ships moored, alive with uniformed men scampering along desks and up masts. Close by was another series of islands, perhaps better described as partially wooded sandstone knolls that ran along the southern shore. The largest seemed to contain a reasonable sized shipyard with dry dock and he wondered if this might be where his brother was employed. Next to the shipyard were a series of sandstone structures that turned out to be a convict penal establishment, a place of secondary punishment for convicts who had re-offended in the colony. Joseph hadn't thought about there still being convicts. He had been told by someone in Rockhampton that the last convict ship to Sydney, the *Eden*, had arrived back in 1840 following a colonial government order to prohibit transportation to the east coast of Australia. He presumed that there had to be people who had been sentenced to long periods, if not life, for their crimes, so logically they could still be deemed as convicts.

Joseph had been amazed at the number of large and beautiful homes that seemed to fill each cove and headland on the harbours southern shore. He was told that people who had struck it rich on the Australian goldfields in the 1850s had bought land along the shore of the harbour and built gracious harbour side homes in which to retire. He noticed some small ferries crisscrossing the harbour, the only access to many of these communities.

As the *Boomerang* turned into Sydney Cove, Joseph observed a large house on the northern shore, its cannons mounted, focussed on the cove's entrance. The captain indicated that the house was the residence of the admiral commanding the British naval squadron stationed in Sydney, he called the building Admiralty House. On a crest of a hill to the west stood a two-storey sandstone tower built in the Italian style. Joseph was fascinated by the two telescope domes and was impressed that the colony obviously had a meteorological station. A fellow passenger told Joseph that at exactly one p.m. a time ball would drop from the top of the tower to signal the correct time to the city below, and at the same time, a cannon was fired from one of the points along the shoreline.

The *Boomerang* was moored about twenty-three metres from a stone wall around the cove that was referred to as Circular Quay. This had been built in the 1850s but with the increased number of ships silting had occurred. To disembark, Joseph had to walk down a heavy ramp connecting the ship to the shore. Behind the reclaimed land that constituted Circular Quay were a large number of warehouses, again bustling with people, goods and wagons of all types. Joseph could see a government building, the Commissariat Store that was used as a Royal Naval store.

Standing on the Quay, Joseph realised he had no idea where the address his brother had sent him was located. Actually, he also didn't know what he looked like. It had been over twenty years since he last saw Thomas, the day his father had left Joseph at the workhouse in Jarrow. He was relieved to see a row of low, two-wheeled carriages, recognising them to be similar to the hansom cabs at home. He entered one, pulling his trunk onto the other side of the seat and spoke to the driver through the trap door at the top. The man grunted but rather than heading toward what appeared to be the centre of the settlement on a well-formed road labelled Pitt Street, he turned the cab in the direction of the hill where Joseph had noticed the observatory. The horse slowly plodded up the steep incline along a road labelled Argyle Street. Toward the top of the rock peninsular the cab passed through a deep rock cutting. Joseph called to the cabbie asking about the cut and in a heavy Yorkshire accent the driver replied that it was called the Argyle Cut and had been dug by convict labour to give better access between Sydney Cove and Millers Point. Joseph looked up at the towering sandstone walls on either side, marks clearly showing the chisel grooves. He felt concern for the men having to cut this out with only hand tools. He imagined men in chain gangs forced to work in the heat, a climate so different from their British homelands.

Once through the cut the cab's pace increased as they headed down the hill towards another cove. This like the one he had left was filled with a variety of sailing ships. Here the cabbie directed Joseph to a wharf where a number of small rowing boats bobbed into the surging tide. Not really knowing what was going on, Joseph loaded his trunk into the small boat, the two oarsmen setting off at pace. The men rowed across a bay then around a point and into another bay that they called Mort Bay. Here there was a noticeable difference, the water darker, almost inky in colour and there were odours of rotting fish, vegetation and noxious gases. Joseph could see a number of shipyards, lumber yards and some small factories, the latter gorging out plumes of black smoke. The banks seemed to be lined with filthy and putrid mud and Joseph could see two large pipes discharging raw sewage directly into the harbour. Sewage floated on the surface of the salt water and appeared to be moving with the tide, but trapped in the cove.

The oarsmen assisted Joseph out of the boat in Balmain and pointed out the way to Alexander Street. Joseph hoisted his trunk on his shoulder and walked the last block, still unsure of his welcome. As it turned out, Thomas was at work but the housekeeper had been informed that eventually his brother Joseph and family might arrive and she was to make them welcome. He was shown to a back bedroom and invited to rest till the family returned.

It was almost dark when Joseph heard the commotion of a father being greeted by his children. The man who knocked and entered the room where Joseph awaited did have some similar features but was taller, had the strong physical build of a person who worked outside, and dark suntanned skin, that made Joseph look anaemic. There was no outpouring of emotion, neither man was comfortable with that, but there was a warm genuine welcome.

Finally meeting his brother, Joseph was saddened to find that his sister-in-law Ann Ross nee Holland had recently died at their home in Alexander Street, Balmain, leaving his brother Thomas with two young daughters to care for, Elizabeth, three, and Florence, two. Ann had died during childbirth of James Ross who died at two months of age. Thomas had also lost another son earlier that year, Thomas H. Ross, aged five.

Despite this loss, Thomas welcomed Joseph into his home as previously discussed in correspondence and showed pleasure at the thought of Christina and Joseph's two remaining children joining them. In some way being together made the joint loss of Thomas's wife and two sons and Joseph's first wife Agnes and son John somehow seem more bearable.

Christina was pleased to leave Rockhampton, it only held sad memories. The children also seemed happy to be moving again, though Agnes was distressed at having to leave her new friends. For Joseph Junior, the highlight was his new clothes. Christina had purchased him two cotton open neck shirts and some long corduroy pants. Though she wasn't sure that Joseph would approve, it seemed to make his son slightly less troublesome.

Being cabin passengers on the *Boomerang,* they had access to their own deck and after a calm voyage down the coast, it is where they stood just after dawn, waiting for the ship to enter though the heads and into Sydney Harbour. A crewman had explained that being steam powered, tide and wind direction was not a concern, but the captain would not enter the harbour till daylight as there were likely to be many small craft and in some parts of the harbour small islands and rock shelves posed a threat.

As the sun rose behind them the enormous headlands, standing boldly before them, changed from a deep brown to a golden glow, the sandstone reflecting the morning sheen. Christina was amazed, they looked so much like the headlands of her childhood home. How much nicer than the mud flats and mangrove swamps that had greeted them in Rockhampton. The air was different as well, clean and fresh, a salty aroma not the rotting vegetation of the tropical north. She guessed the heads to be over a mile wide.

The children screamed with delight when a pod of dolphin began surfing in the ship's wake. Once through the heads, Christina could visualise the enormity of this enclosed bay. Between ridges that flowed down to the water's edge, small crescent-shaped beaches of bright yellow sand were being peacefully lapped by rows of small waves. The gathered passengers looked skyward as a flock of birds with bold pink plumage darted overhead. A fellow passenger called them pink galahs then pointed to the bank where a screeching noise could be heard.

'Those noisy fellas are cockatoos.'

These birds were bigger, with white plumage and yellow feathers on their heads. Christina looked around her, the hillsides covered with green vegetation, the sparking water, little boats bobbing in the swell, fishermen intent on their catch, truly this had to be the most beautiful harbour in the world.

The *Boomerang* docked on the eastern side of a semi-circular cove lined with other ships. Most were tall-mast clipper ships, and to the west appeared to be rows of warehouses. She had sighted Joseph long before the gangplank was lowered and guessed the man standing next to him had to be his brother, Thomas. The children were excited to see their father, running ahead to greet him. Her greeting more subdued, having not seen him since before their son's death.

The men led them along a wide dirt road that ran along the edge of a stone embankment to where two sailing boats were waiting. Joseph had explained that Thomas had insisted on collecting Christina and the children by boat and that he and one of his workers had brought Joseph with them on the morning tide. Once their trunks were loaded they set sail heading further into the harbour. Joseph Junior was ecstatic when Thomas offered to let him steer the boat. Though Joseph protested, Thomas insisted.

Over the next few days, Thomas enjoyed telling the new arrivals stories about his new homeland. One Christina was rather concerned about was the number of bushrangers that Thomas talked about having been shot in the last twelve months. Dan Morgan, who they called "Mad Dog" and was considered one of the most bloodthirsty of colonial freebooters. Ben Hall and John Gilbert, a member of Ben Hall's gang. Britain had its highwaymen, but these sounded much worse. Thomas had copies of the local newspaper, the *Bell's Life in Sydney and Sporting Chronicle*, that he had kept for Joseph to get a feel of what was happening in the colony.

# Chapter 15

Though eager to start his own business Joseph had neither the capital nor contacts, thus accepted a position working for James Alexander Brown at the Sydney Glassworks in Kersey Lane (later named Little Dixon Street). He was employed as a bottle maker, charged with making carboys, also called demijohn, a large rigid container and soda bottles. Brown supplied the capital and Ross the knowhow.

Though the first glass made in Australia had come from the glassworks owned by Simeon Lord and Francis Williams at Pyrmont, in 1812, the owners found difficulties working with their manager, "professor" Hutchison and had abandoned the venture.

Joseph wanted this new venture to be a success, so sought help in identifying suitable raw materials to make quality bottles. He developed a friendship with a professor at Sydney University by the name of Morris Birkbeck Pell. Though born in Illinois in America, his mother had moved to England where he attended St John's College, Cambridge. Pell's grandfather, Morris Birkbeck, had been an English

Quaker agricultural innovator, social reformer and antislavery campaigner. He had founded a utopian colony, the English Settlement, in Illinois where Morris had been born.

In 1852 Pell had been chosen from twenty-six candidates as the first professor of mathematics and natural philosophy at Sydney University. Pell assisted Joseph in the testing of quality of furnaces and fireclays resistant to high temperatures and therefore suitable for lining furnaces and identifying other appropriate local raw materials.

Besides his university work, Pell had a range of skills and knowledge. He was the chairman of a commission to enquire into the surveyor-general's department in 1855, a member of the commission on a fatal railway accident in 1858, and chairman of the commission on methods of testing marine steam-boilers in 1868. He was also chairman of the Sydney City and Suburban Sewage and Health Board 1875–77. In 1870 he became a director and consulting actuary for the Mutual Life Association of Australasia.

Throughout his business life Joseph maintained a close friendship with Morris, often seeking his advice and the business links he could provide.

Christina had enjoyed the company of Morris' wife Jane and visited their home in Glebe. As the Pell's had five boys and three girls their house was always filled with noise, but often not happy. On one visit, Jane informed Christina that she was taking some of the children to live in Tasmania. Christina was shocked when told by Joseph that on his death, Morris had left an annuity of eighty pounds to his estranged wife, provided she did not return to Sydney.

At Joseph's insistence Christina had attended Morris' funeral in 1879 but found going to the Balmain cemetery very stressful as it held memories of her own previous losses.

# Chapter 16

While Joseph was very busy establishing himself Christina found she had a growing curiosity about the new city she found herself living in. Though British, it was very different from the city life she had experienced in Edinburgh. Joseph never felt like exploring, he was always working or planning, but Thomas who used to take long evening walks with his wife, enjoyed chaperoning Christina as she explored the city. Being hilly, Christina was pleased that her wire cage frame skirt with layers of petticoats had been replaced by crinoline. This new clothing style released the wearer from the weight and voluminous underskirts of previous fashions. A sensible, though full, skirt and waist length jacket, high laced boots, bonnet and parasol were far more suitable on cobblestone streets, dirt minor roads and the grass surface of parks and gardens.

Their initial walks had been on the Balmain peninsular, though it was not a pretty place as industry was taking a hold of the foreshore. The once attractive Waterview Bay on the north side of the Balmain Peninsular, which had a small stream feeding into it from the Balmain Hills, had become an ever-expanding dry dock. An industrialist Mort and former steamship captain, T.S. Roundtree, had purchased the land in 1854. In competition with the government dry dock at Cockatoo Island they developed Mort's Dock. Mort and Roundtree had then leased most of the surrounding land for cargo storage, engineering works and an iron and brass foundry. Once seen as an elite area, the earlier settlers objected to the pollution and blocking of their marine views. Thomas really couldn't complain as the growth helped both his shipwright business and his own fledgling shipyard.

Before long, the focus of their walks became the city itself with its extensive parks and gardens. On several occasion the outing began with a ride on horse-bus 158 which was one of several buses operating from the Balmain Peninsular carrying passengers to the city centre via the recently opened Glebe Island Bridge. However, Thomas, being a shipwright, had done both repair and building work for the local ferry company owner and as part of the agreement he and his family were granted free travel on the ferries.

Perdriau Ferries had been established by Henry Perdriau who ran a ferry from the Darling Street Ferry Wharf, Balmain to the Australian Gas Light Company Wharf at Millers Point. The gas company had established on the edge of the harbour in 1837 with its gas holding tanks hewn out of the foreshore's solid sandstone. Given a royal charter, the company supplied town gas for Sydney's first public lighting of lamps in 1841 to celebrate the birthday of Queen Victoria.

The first steamer, *Waterman*, had commenced in February 1844. Prior to this, a service was offered on demand in small rowing skiffs or sailing dinghies.

Following a short but pleasant ferry ride, though sometimes industrial smells and floating debris in the water detracted from the scene, they would head off. Their walk normally commenced with a stroll south along the Darling Harbour shoreline then cutting through on a side lane into the city centre or to either the Botanic Gardens or Hyde Park.

Christina enjoyed looking through the front display windows of the fine shops along Pitt Street, between King and Market Streets. Though still a mix of single and multi-storey buildings the quality and array of things for sale were dazzling. She was sure the shopping here was far superior to that of Edinburgh. However, one of her favourite shops was in the parallel George Street.

The Café Francaise boasted little marble tables, fine food, reading material such as *The Times*, chessboards and even billiards. As the café was licensed to sell alcohol, they didn't enter but Christina could tell that Thomas had, and perhaps was a regular visitor, as several of the waiters addressed him by name.

They often opted to stroll along the hilly Macquarie Street as it appeared to hold the finest houses in the town. All looked so grand, some up to four storeys high. One summer evening, they stayed longer than usual to see the street come to life in the background of an orange glow of the setting sun, in the west. The large windows, many framed in rich crimson curtains from where a glow of light and music could be heard flowing from upper storey music rooms. Ladies dressed in evening clothes sat on verandas, draped on beautiful couches. It was a wonderful sight and Christina smiled as she thought of the drab greys of her childhood Wick.

Thomas seemed to know his city very well. As they walked through Wynyard Square, he pointed out the smart townhouses which had been built after the army vacated the land when it had moved to the Victoria Barracks at Paddington in 1848. He mentioned that the area had a high Jewish merchant population, but this meant little to Christina as she didn't know of any Jewish people in Wick and her father had not mentioned any specific contact with them.

From what she had seen, Christina had deduced that the successful merchants, shopkeepers and professional people seemed to live in mansions and villas, mainly on higher land, and on the edge of the city, such as Paddington, Darlinghurst and Glebe. Certainly, the same had to be said for Macquarie

Street and Lower Fort Street. The skilled workers and thus middle class, seemed to have four- or five-roomed houses in districts such as Balmain, Pyrmont, Surry Hills and Redfern. From their walks she thought some of the upper Rocks and Millers Point would also fall into this type of area. She was aware of the rapid growth of smaller workers houses close to the expending industrial concentrations, but other parts of the city, were certainly some of the worst she had seen. Once Thomas had taken her through the lower reaches of the Rocks. Here conditions seemed almost squalid, many structures barely huts or caves. Sadly, it reminded her of the Tinker Caves in the cliffs at Wick. Wretched people, poorly dressed, undernourished, crammed into an impoverished life. Thomas had made it very clear that she and her family should stay away from these streets and lanes as he felt they were filled with thieves and violent gangs.

A far more pleasant part of the city to visit was the Botanic Gardens. Christina was struck by the natural beauty of the place with its interesting exhibits like the zoo and aviary. They strolled down the shady avenue lined with Morton Bay figs and read a small sign indicating they had only been planted in 1847. However, they were already huge, this prime location overlooking the harbour obviously suited them. Together, Christina and Thomas would sit, resting at a place called Mrs Macquarie's Chair. It was an actual bench that had been hand carved out of a sandstone rock ledge by convicts in 1810. It had been commissioned by her husband, Major-General Lachlan Macquarie, governor of the New South Wales colony, as his wife Elizabeth loved the area and had expressed her belief that it had one of the best vantage points to view Sydney. How Christina wished that Joseph would do these walks with her, he was a dutiful husband but in some ways removed, preoccupied with "more important things." A few times, not thinking, she had held Thomas's hand as they sat together, he never pulled back, also enjoying the caring contact. She felt guilty that she was enjoying his company more and more. Each day she was delighted to see him, they had long conversations about what was going on in the colony, even a little gossip. He would comment on her appearance or the skill of her handicraft, something that Joseph would never think to do.

Their walks in Hyde Park were also relaxing but less impressive. Basically until 1854 the area had been common land mainly used for grazing. There were some tracks and dirt roads, one called the Racetrack, as locals raced their horses there. In 1854 the Public Park Act was passed, and the Hyde Park Improvement Committee was formed. Christina laughed when Thomas told her their aim was to make the park more bourgeois, to create a decorative open space for middle class strolling, just as they were doing.

As they walked, Thomas seemed to know and speak to every second person. Christina was always introduced as his brother's wife with the mention that Joseph had immigrated to the colony to establish a bottle making business. This seemed to impress most of these well-dressed strangers and several women gave Christina their calling cards. They were pulled deftly out of drawstring purses with the accompanying request for Christina to call on them for tea. Christina realised that this very British custom was still the way things were done among certain classes in the colony so decided that she too needed to get some cards made, checking with Thomas that it was acceptable to use his address.

Christina wasn't sure how Joseph would react to this level of social contact but was both surprised and pleased when he was very supportive. They both knew that establishing links and networks was essential for any successful business. Though he had the technical skills, he was unknown, and initially was just another skilled trade person working for a local businessman.

Christina was surprised that most of the cards she had been handed were from women who were either in business in their own right or were working with their husbands.

Mrs Theresa Burridge had a confectioner's licence and a premises on Pitt Street in her own name. Her husband Isaac North had suddenly died in 1864 and she had also assumed control of his well-established ginger beer manufacturing. Joseph saw her as an excellent contact.

Mrs Dick owned her own house and also owned the coach house next door. She hired out her coaches, employing local men as drivers.

Miss Lee was partners with her sister in a straw hat/bonnet making business. When they emigrated, they had owned a similar business in Staffordshire, England.

Miss Margaret Doak had emigrated from Ireland and with her sister owned a milliner and dressmaking business.

Christina enjoyed the company of Mary Brereton, wife of Dr Brereton, who had set up a dispensary in Sydney and had also opened Sydney's first Turkish bath in Spring Street, formerly the Captain Cook Hotel. Dr Brereton has set up his practice in Macquarie Street and Joseph saw the potential in the manufacture of glass containers for all types of medicines. Though Christina liked Mary she found her husband, or at least some of his ideas too different from her own. He became the leader of the New Jerusalem Church in Sydney, he advocated for cremation, rational clothing for men but side stepped any changes in the traditional expectations placed on women.

There was also Louise Dutruc who was to become both a contact and friend. Louise and her husband Pierre had emigrated after teaching French in Glasgow for twelve years. Pierre also owned a wine and spirit business and was the author of a French grammar book. They were considered a highly respectable couple both teaching French at various local private academies. Christina enjoyed sitting for hours chatting and regaining her confidence in the language. Pierre was considered by Joseph as an important contact, he was on the city council for Randwick and acted as the French consul so knew many people in trade and shipping.

# Chapter 17

On a crisp but sunny morning, Thomas informed Joseph he would be taking his eighteen-foot sailing boat out to deliver a smaller boat recently completed for a customer. He wondered if he and Christina might enjoy a day on the water as his delivery would involve sailing along the southern shore of the harbour. Joseph again indicated he was too busy but if Christina wished to go, he had no objections. Though her pregnancy was beginning to show, she was excited at the opportunity.

The children were to be left under the care of the housemaid, Isabel, and Thomas assured Mrs Connelly his cook they would be home in time for supper. She quickly placed some freshly baked bread, cheese and cold meat in linen, for their lunch. Thomas protested that the people to whom he was delivering the boat to would offer them food, but Mrs Connelly insisted.

Thomas and Christina walked to his boatyard where two of his workmen were waiting. The four sailed the two boats from Mort Bay on the outward tide. Keeping south of Goat Island, they sailed towards the ocean heads passing Walsh Bay then Sydney Cove. Christina could see a mixture of tall sailing ships and some more modern steamships that were fast becoming the preferred method of moving people and cargo. There were several ferries that tooted their horns as their engines revved past. Rounding the point on which the Botanic Gardens stood, Christina could see the new Government House with the city as its backdrop. Thomas pointed out their special place, the carved bench at the tip of the peninsular. They continued eastward towards Shark Island, but the number of vessels had diminished, and most were now smaller sail and rowing boats. They tacked north, closer to the heads, then around a point heading south again into a large bay that Thomas called Vaucluse Bay. As the bay narrowed Christina could see a large house in Gothic Revival style with extensive gardens looming towards them. She was impressed by the main structure plus a number of outbuildings which she assumed were servant quarters, stables and based on the smoke rising from several chimneys, a kitchen wing.

Thomas's boat glided onto a sandy beach where several rowing boats were beached, and three men stood waiting. From their dress, two were servants, the other she assumed the farm's owner. He looked in his mid-thirties, was tall, with thick shoulders, a Roman shaped nose with masses of auburn hair. He directed the two younger men to assist Christina and to her shock, one lifted her out of the boat, carrying her across the sand and grass to a stony path. She blushed with embarrassment, her outer skit filling like a sail in the breeze. The young man though thin and wiry was so strong, he also seemed amused at her dilemma, his muscular arms holding her close to his body as she wiggled and squirmed. She realised she was actually lucky he had not dropped her, imagining the first impression that would have made.

A young woman approached, dressed in a skirt, jacket and cap, who Christina assumed was a maid. The girl who appeared to be in her late teens, with a heavy Irish brogue, politely invited her to join her mistress in the drawing-room. Christina suddenly realised that she didn't even know the name of her host. Thomas had referred to William and Sarah but that was all. She turned back to ask Thomas but he, and she presumed William, were already on-board William's new boat discussing timber and sails.

Nearing the house, Christina could see two men working in the very formal, English garden, the path to the house almost a labyrinth. Both men looked up and smiled but Christina realised it was the servant girl who their attention was focussed on. All the servants seemed so tanned and looked so fit and healthy. These two were older, their faces ravaged by time yet they moved so freely carrying large, heavy looking rocks that they were using to create a terrace wall.

Beyond the formal lawn surrounding a fountain an attractive, thin faced middle-aged women stood on a shaded veranda, her green dress voluminous over traditional hooping. After a warm welcome, where the woman just called herself Sarah, Christina was shown into the drawing room. The space Christina considered equal to about the complete downstairs of Thomas's house. The walls were decorated in floral wallpaper, there were large plaster cornices and a marble fire surround and cast iron grate. When Christina commented on the beautiful furnishings, Sarah told her that they had recently replaced all the original furniture with items they had purchased in Europe when they were living there.

Over tea served in the finest china Christina had ever seen, and plates of cakes and tarts, the women discussed their children and husbands. Sarah pointed to a painting of her son Fitzwilliam who was a lawyer, like his father, had studied at Cambridge University in England but now had a property near Dunedin in New Zealand. She went on to say he was currently visiting her, and it was him that Christina had seen on the beach. Sarah apologised that her husband was not there to meet her, but he had returned to England on business.

There was a painting of her daughter Sarah, but with sadness in her eyes the woman added that she had passed away a few years earlier while they were vacationing in Corfu, Greece. Christina expressed empathy to Sarah explaining she had also lost a child, her son John.

The painting of her daughter Thomasine was of a beautiful woman with bright orange hair. Sarah explained she had married a Mr Fishes and now had her own family.

The painting of William II was of another youth with reddish hair, and also had a black ribbon draped across the top of the frame. Sarah explained that William had hearing and sight problems and though he entered university in England to become a lawyer, had become ill and passed away.

The painting of a young soldier was Sarah's son D'Arcy. He had been educated at Harrow in England then attended Sandhurst. Sarah seemed proud that he was an officer in the King's Royal Irish Hussars and was posted in Scotland. Discussion following this was about Christina's family links with the Sinclairs in northern Scotland. Sarah seemed genuinely interested about Christina's heritage.

There was also a black ribbon on a picture of Isabella, a painting of Edith, and a painting of Laura. Christina could tell that Sarah, like most mothers, was very proud of her children and their achievements.

Several times Christina indicated she should find Thomas as they had to sail back to Balmain and Thomas had told her they needed to sail with the tides.

Each time Sarah raised a new topic, she seemed not only to be enjoying Christina's company but not wanting her to leave. Finally, the same maid informed her mistress that her son had sent her to fetch Christina as Thomas was ready to leave. Sarah thanked Christina for her visit, saying how much she enjoyed their time together, almost pleading with her to come again.

Christina recounted her experiences to Thomas during the voyage home. He didn't seem surprised and explained despite all William Wentworth's achievements, their beautiful estate and wealth, the family had struggled to gain acceptance in Sydney society. He went on to talk about their social exclusion due to the fact that they were both children of convicts and perhaps worst, their first two children were born before they were married. Thomas knew some of the family's history and how they had lived and had their children educated in Europe between 1853 and 1861.

Thomas liked William, he saw him as a talented and outspoken lawyer and campaigner for social equality in the colony. He stressed that of nearly all persons he had met, William had done the most to counter the civil barriers between free settlers and convict descendants. Thomas remembered a hurtful article he had read in an 1847 *Sydney Morning Herald* that had said of Sarah Wentworth nee. Cox:

"Whenever a woman falls, she falls forever… She becomes, as it, were socially dead."

Christina could now see why this elegant, and she considered, superior woman, had gone to such trouble with the wife of a glass blower, but importantly, a free settler. She resolved to call on her again and if she could help break down this divide, she would do whatever she could.

Christina was fascinated about the Wentworths and managed to find that William had been born on the vessel HMS *Surprize* off the coast of the penal settlement, Norfolk Island. His mother Catherine Crowley was a convict who had become pregnant to D'Arcy Wentworth, a member of a wealthy and aristocratic Anglo-Irish family. D'Arcy had been tried four times for highway robbery but eventually, to avoid prosecution, had accepted the position of assistant surgeon in the colony of New South Wales. William's parents had become prosperous landowners at Parramatta and William had been sent to a private school in England. In 1813 along with George Blaxland and William Lawson, William had found a route over the Blue Mountains. In 1827 when his father had died leaving him a small fortune he purchased Vaucluse, an estate on the south shore of Sydney Harbour. He had married in 1829.

Sarah Cox was the daughter of two convicts both transported from England for theft. She had been a milliner and met William when he acted as her lawyer

in a case where she sued a Captain Payne for breach
of promise of marriage.

127

# Chapter 18

Only nine months later, Joseph's brother Thomas remarried. Isabel, also surnamed Ross, came from Richmond, a town in the Hawkesbury River Valley. She was the daughter of a convict, Charles Ross, who had arrived as one of three hundred and twenty convicts on the *Marquis of Huntley,* arriving in 1835, sentenced to seven years at the Perth Court of Justice. At the time, he had been a shoemaker's boy, aged fifteen, and was charged with robbing the till. He had gained his Certificate of Freedom in 1842. Charles had been employed as a labourer working on one of the corn farms in the Richmond area. The river's flood plain, rich alluvial soil, grew large amounts of wheat and corn and Richmond boasted two flour mills run by George Howell and William Bowman. Farming, however, was difficult due to regular major flooding.

Isabel had come to work as a servant in the Ross household. Each day she wore a calico dress either purple or moss green and a white bonnet. She was a quiet girl who went about her duties showing respect to Christina, who had taken on the role of carer for the four children and the Ross brothers.

Though Christina was only five years older than Isabel, it seemed they were worlds apart. Christina was educated where Isabel had limited home schooling. Christina had lost a child, and was now eight months pregnant, and Isabel was just turning nineteen and lacked worldly knowledge. Christina's stepdaughter Agnes at nine seemed to share more interests and sensibilities with Isabel, but Isabel was very good with the children, playing games and making up stories to amuse them.

A few days after the marriage, Christina was in the kitchen discussing with the cook the purchase of food for the children's meals. Isabel was standing at the door listening. Both women were surprised when Isabel intervened.

'I'm the mistress of the house now, Mrs Ross is a guest in my home and her opinion is no longer required.'

The shocked look on both women's faces did not deter her.

'You spend far too much on fancy foods, they're not necessary, good plain food from now on.'

The cook looked pleadingly at Christina but she could do nothing, not saying a word she left the kitchen and opted to go for a long walk. Christina pondered on what had happened. Had Isabel resented her closeness to Thomas, their long walks, and the fact that on many evening Joseph would retire early, after a hard day's work, leaving them sitting at the dining table? Here they would often spend hours sharing stories from the paper or talking of gossip they had been told.

That look on Isabel's face, a hard, angry demeanour that she had not previously displayed.

Dinner that night was in silence, Thomas tried several times to talk to Christina but Isabel would interrupt. The stew served was thick and tasteless. The cook's revenge, Christina thought. Though Joseph cleared his plate, Thomas and Christina just picked at the chunky vegetables.

'It's what Mrs Ross instructed me to make,' the cook said, glaring at Isabel. 'There's a big pot so you will be eating it for a few nights. Healthy plain food, Mrs Ross insisted on helping me cook it herself.'

'I'm not really hungry,' Thomas finally said.

'A client invited Christina and I to lunch today so we both had a hearty meal then.'

Though Joseph was oblivious to her reaction, Isabel glared at Christina and announced she was going to bed. Thomas followed, not realising what had happened. When they retired, Christina told Joseph about Isabel's comments and at her insistence he promised to find alternative accommodation as soon as possible.

The next morning, Thomas was apologetic, indicating that Isabel was unwell and had asked if

Christina could take the children to the park. A new maid had not been employed to replace Isabel and that had been one of her previous duties.

Two days later, Joseph and his family moved into a single-storey masonry house at 17 Dixon Street, at the northwest corner of Kersey's Lane. The lane that led to the timber and brick glass factory where he worked ran down the side of their home. The house was smaller than Thomas's, its furniture old and sparse. While Joseph was at work, Christina set about making curtains, whitewashing the walls and establishing a small vegetable garden. She now had three children to look after but Agnes, who missed her cousins Elizabeth and Florence, was very good at helping with her new half-brother, baby Thomas.

Though Joseph's two children had started to attend a school in Rockhampton, Christina was now expected to provide home schooling for Agnes and Joseph. Though Agnes was eager to learn, Joseph Junior struggled with his lessons and became belligerent, and at each attempted session was hostile and aggressive. Christina noted he tended to be hyperactive and impulsive. He had a very short attention span and was easily distracted. Both at his schooling and with jobs he was asked to do in the house or garden he made careless mistakes. While Joseph and Christina were both thorough in all their planning, Joseph Junior had difficulty in organising tasks, resulting in both his parents commenting on his forgetfulness. As a family they didn't have much but it frustrated Christina that Joseph Junior would often lose things and didn't seem to care.

# Chapter 19

Though Christina had found solace with the Primitive Methodist preacher and congregation in Rockhampton, she was surprised and disappointed with the mission in Sydney. The church's administration was based in Melbourne and Sydney was attached to it. Delegates from the Sydney circuit had to travel one thousand two hundred miles to attend district meetings. In 1865, poor attendance and administration had resulted in Sydney being downgraded to mission status. In 1871, the Sydney District only had eight hundred and fifteen members, but this slowly grew and in 1901 the number had grown to two thousand and thirty-six.

The first missions to the colonies had commenced in 1843 when Primitive Methodist missionaries followed the tide of emigration from Great Britain. In 1835, the European settlers in the Australian colonies numbered eighty thousand, but by 1851 this had risen to three hundred and fifty thousand. With the discovery of gold, between 1853 and 1855, one million three hundred thousand emigrants left British ports for Australia. In 1840 a group of Primitive

Methodists gathered together in Adelaide, the major settlement in the South Australian colony. At their open-air meeting they pledged to form their own society. One of their group donated some land on which the first Australian Primitive Methodist chapel was built. By the beginning of 1841, the group had sixteen members, four preachers and twenty-two children attending their Sabbath School.

John Wilson travelled from Adelaide to Sydney in 1847 to set up a mission there. Unfortunately, the men who took up the lead proved to be of questionable character and their reputations resulted in the failure of the first attempts to establish the church. In 1849 E. Tear was sent from England but also struggled to encourage the remaining faithful but eventually managed to get a small chapel built. In conflict with the basic beliefs of the religion, he had a strong belief in patriarchy, dismissing the ideas and opinions expressed by women.

In 1854 when John Sharpe was sent from England, he found only one hundred and sixteen members in the Sydney mission. Over the next fifteen years at the Sydney mission, he would oversee the community's growth.

Christina respected John, he was always straightforward and conscientious. She found him to have a strong will and quick mind. This was a quality she found lacking in many of those in authority in the mission. She enjoyed reading his articles in the *New*

*South Wales Primitive Methodist Messenger,* though she didn't realise at the time that part of his mission was to use his pen to deliberately vindicate Primitive Methodism though the press. He spent time trying to counter some of the mismanagement and misinformation of ministers who had done good works in England but were pursuing a divisive policy in the colony. Strongly anti-Pope, they spent their time undermining others rather than growing their own flock.

One thing that Christina had noted was that colonial society had a levelling effect, the difference between the Primitive and Wesleyan Methodist tended to be diminished by their shared colonial experiences and challenges. This seemed to apply to all aspects of colonial life. From its convict beginnings, European settlement had struggled with a totally different demographic and financial base compared to life in Europe. Protestants made up a significant proportion of the government but many of the convicts and early emigrants were Catholic. Distance became a major factor in that most of the preachers were young, the majority lay, and were not bound and controlled by the central British religious hierarchy. Where in Britain, the churches dominated social and economic affairs, the colony was seen as a new freedom, and an opportunity to break away from class-based rules and restrictions.

After 1858, almost every male over the age of twenty-one had the right to vote. Up till then only male landowners could vote. Even after 1858 there were disparities in electorates. Pastoral districts had one representative per three thousand voters but in the city, it was one representative per five thousand nine hundred voters, thus pastoralist votes technically were worth twice as much as city dwellers. Also, very few people could afford to stand for election as members were not paid until 1889. As elections took place over a period of weeks, if a person lost in one seat, they had time to stand for another electorate as there was no rule regarding having to live in or have any business links with, the electorate that you stood for. As the NSW State Parliament met for up to ten months a year many farmers could not afford to be away from their homes during busy times like harvest and shearing thus rural electorates tended to be held by city lawyers and merchants. Joseph often talked about standing for local council or state parliament, but Christina knew that would not happen, he was too devoted to his work and would not be able to spare the time.

Christina considered religion in the colony to be like a child, it inherited the traits of its parents but adapted to the environment in which it found itself. Where in Europe the establishment had planned development, religion in the colonies tended to result from like-minded people forming a group, then requesting a preacher whose role was seen more as a coordinator, preaching, Sabbath School teaching, and nurturing the growing membership. Often when the preachers were appointed, they were young and inexperienced and relied on the wisdom, experience and practical help of the laity. This resulted in the diluting of pastoral supremacy, something Christina felt was good for both the church and the people who attended it. She also liked the way the Primitive church was more flexible, willing to bend and change to reflect community needs and expectations. Time and dates for meeting would be modified to fit the season and local conveniences. Meetings also added an element of social gathering and even light entertainment, depending on the group's evangelical approach.

Christina watched as faces changed, both where she lived, and in the city as a whole. Where Scottish and English society reflected a continuity of location and lengthy development of social networks, here there was a mobile population, people just left, free to search for the next, better opportunity. Some of this was large scale such as the massive flows connected with gold discoveries, but some were just people looking for a better job or building to live in. She found that British stability and continuity, with all its faults, lacking.

The colony had taken some of its own steps to support the establishment of permanent institutions.

In 1836, the New South Wales colonial government had passed the Church Act. This gave state aid to churches and parsonages and minister's stipends. This act had established legally the principle of religious equality in the colony, another aspect of her new homeland she felt would eventually lead to a less combative society.

# Chapter 20

In August 1866 Joseph made the first bottle in Australia. A blown bottle, using a clay mould that Christina had shaped for him.

While Joseph had been developing the furnace and glass house pots, Christina spent months working with clay, fashioning moulds, a range of shapes and sizes into which the melted glass could be poured then blown to shape using a metal pipe. As it would turn out, their son Thomas was born at Dixon Street on the same night his father first fashioned a bottle in Sydney.

The moulds that Christina made allowed the molten glass to be blown to fill the mould then withdrawn vertically, thus the power in the process was supplied by human lung capacity. The moulds allowed for the production of bottles of uniform size and shape. Christina also developed the moulds so as to allow words, such as who the bottle was made for and by whom, to be included on the bottle. Once lifted from the mould the finish, a rim, was still completed by hand, tongs used to ensure uniform finishing.

At the 1866–67 Intercolonial and International Exhibition held in Melbourne, a bottle blown by Joseph was awarded a prize medal. However, as the business was owned by James Brown, he was awarded the prize, presented eight days before the exhibition closed. Neither Joseph nor Brown could afford the time or expense of attending but were eager to use the award to publicise their success.

The exhibition brought together exhibits to assist in the selection of items to be forwarded to Paris for the Exposition Universelle. It was the first time the Australian colonies had come together to demonstrate the farming, industrial and social advancement occurring in this new land. In addition, there were exhibitors from New Zealand, New Caledonia, Mauritius, Netherland and India. Each colony had been assigned a specific area, or "court", competition between the colonies obvious.

There was a total of six hundred and forty-eight medallions produced to be awarded to exhibits of excellence. Though there were two thousand nine hundred and fifty-six exhibitors, the majority were Victorian. The exhibits were assessed by thirty-nine juries.

For Christina and Joseph, this success was a confirmation that between them they had both the skills and technology to commence production of bottles in the colony. The raw materials required were found in abundance and were of high quality.

# Chapter 21

In late 1866, Joseph left his employment with Brown and formed a partnership called Blackburn and Company, set up with William Wilthew and Robert Blackburn who had supplied the capital.

They rented a small property in Balmain close to Darling Street wharves to allow access to the large quantity of coal and sand needed in production. The property also had two stone cottages, one of which became the Ross family home. Though busy helping in the factory, Christina had three children in her care, thus her stepdaughter Agnes, at the age of 9, took on the day-to-day care of Joseph and Thomas. The factory was completed by December, basically a large timber shed with galvanised iron roof with bricks used for chimney and furnace.

Though Christina understood the reason for the location, she was concerned about the morals of the area. With her temperance background, living in an area referred to as the Sandstone Hotel Precinct was less than satisfactory. The area was the largest residential area of the colony and housed about twenty percent of Sydney's population. It was predominantly working class as workers wanted to be close to where the industrial work was available. When taking the children for a daily walk she passed a range of alcohol outlets including the Shipwright Arms at 10 Darling Street built 1844, the Unity Hall Hotel, 49 Darling Street built 1848 and Waterford Arms 50 Darling Street built 1846. No matter the time of day, intoxicated men spilled out of the pubs, some calling out offensive comments.

She had learnt, after marriage, that Joseph, though still having Wesleyan Methodist leanings, sometimes liked to imbibe, a private whisky to celebrate or when he felt overwhelmed by life. Despite this, in his first business with Blackburn and Wilthew, he had been black and white, encouraged by Christina, that the business adopted a policy of not making any containers that would be used to hold alcohol.

Though there was an obvious demand for their product, the Balmain glasswork site was forced to close by the Balmain Municipal Authority with the introduction of the Smoke Nuisance Prevention Act. Many of the new residents had complained, writing to the council about the noise and soot that billowed from the chimneys, covering their washing and putting a layer of ash over everything. Their complaints were not just focussed on the glassworks but at the range of industries that were located near the wharves. The area was changing, there was a transition from the small plain style homes of the 1840s to the ornate grandeur of the 1860s reflecting the growing prosperity of the colony.

Though Joseph lodged petitions referring to loss of employment and economic opportunities the partnership was forced to declare bankruptcy on 20th February 1867. This upset Joseph, as he perceived the failure was not his fault. He slumped into a type of depression, aware that the bankruptcy could tarnish the Ross name. Christina now found herself in the role of supporter and encourager. She was surprised that Joseph seem to almost fall apart at the loss. Previously he had been so positive of his abilities and almost oblivious to criticism or the opinions of others. She had experienced his self-absorption when left in Rockhampton to deal with the loss of John, so now saw a weakness that had not been there before.

Though he had initially resented the fact that Blackburn had insisted that the business be advertised in his name, after all Joseph and Christina were the ones who had the skills and did the work, Christina convinced him to be thankful for that arrangement. To suppliers and customers Joseph was considered just an employee, a journeyman, presumably paid cash, thus removed from public blame.

Joseph gained a Certificate of Discharge in October 1867. To make a living, Christina encouraged him to return to work blowing glass at the Dixon Street glassworks but by this time it was owned by John Longford.

Though the factory was closed the family initially remained in the onsite cottage.

# Chapter 22

In the 1860s and early 1870s the economy was in a boom period, mostly due to income from the gold rushes, the wool industry and growing manufacturing and construction sectors. An acute shortage of labour, despite the steady influx of migrants, pushed wages up to the highest in the world. The term "working man's paradise" was used to describe the opportunities in the colonies.

In 1868, Joseph was behind the issuing of a prospectus for the formation of the Australian Glass Co. Ltd. The plan was for a new factory in Camperdown, financed through the sale of two thousand five hundred shares at two pounds each. In the prospectus, a dramatic shift in Joseph's values can be detected. Prior to this, he had publicly followed the beliefs of his Methodist faith and outwardly supported the temperance movement, not willing to blow containers for brewers, distillers and vintners. The new company planned on focussing its production on Württemberg hock bottles 'especially adapted to the requirements of the colony's wine growers and bottlers.' Though the company had on its proposed board a banker, magistrate, builder and politician, Joseph seemed to be the only one with any glass industry knowledge. The prospectus did not attract enough interest for the company to go ahead but at the same time Joseph had gained finance from Benjamin Lattin, a spirit merchant and businessman from Nattai near Mittagong. An 1868 listing in the Sands Sydney Directory referred to the Lattin Glassworks, Camperdown Road, Joseph Ross, glassblower.

Joseph had chosen to shift his Methodist beliefs further from Primitive and more to Wesleyan. He would cite one of Wesley's 1780 pamphlets *A Word to a Drunkard*, which described spirituous liquors as poison and links drunkenness with adultery, murder and all manner of villainies. However, Wesley recommended beer to his preachers to sustain them between preaching, as it was a source of calories, and sometimes safer to drink than water. Joseph felt that Wesley's call for temperance was more literal, from the Latin noun *temperantia* and verb *temperare*, meaning moderation and self-restraint.

Lattin was a former wholesale grocer in Melbourne who had leased the Fitzroy Iron Works, near Mittagong, in early 1863. He had agreed to construct a blast furnace, at his own expense, in return for shares in the company. Lattin was given a twelve-month lease on the local iron ore mines and the company had the prospect of a contract to manufacture railway tracks. While the furnace was being built, Lattin organised for the purchase of scrap metal to be rerolled into rail track and by 1863 track was being produced at the rate of thirty-six tons per week. The works advertised for limestone and for coalminers to work the coal outcrop at Nattai Gorge. Because of delays in the construction of the blast furnace, Lattin's contract ran out. In 1865, Lattin was managing the City Iron Works in Sydney, which was also rerolling scrap iron into railway track.

The New South Wales colonial government introduced Stamp Duty in 1865, a tax levied on single property purchases or documents. A physical revenue stamp now had to be attached to all cheques, receipts, licences and land transactions. This was adding another cost to business and both Lattin and Ross attended a public meeting to protest what they saw as an unnecessary government invasion into business freedom. It is here they met for the first time, and it was Lattin who approached Joseph about the future of glass manufacturing. Lattin expressed the same opinion as Joseph and agreed to finance him in a new glass bottle manufacturing venture. Again, when the business was established, it was named for its financier.

Christina, who was developing into an astute businesswoman, quickly convinced Benjamin Lattin that it was the Ross name that customers respected, both for quality and reliability, thus he agreed to it being changed. She was concerned that he was an opportunist, trying to take advantage of Joseph's need for capital. This was to prove a shrewd move, as by the beginning of October 1869, Lattin was being sued for unpaid bills. His reputation and name were also brought into question when it was reported he had been killed in November 1869. The report described his death as gruesome, killed aboard a French-protectorate flagged barque, in Fiji, when about to depart for Queensland. The report implied that out of financial desperation, he had become involved in "blackbirding". This was a disguised form of slavery, and one of his victims had killed him. Blackbirding involved the coercion or kidnapping of people to work as poorly paid labourers, such as used on the sugarcane fields of Queensland. These "blackbirded" people were called Kanaks, the term originally referring to native Hawaiians.

# Chapter 23

Christina gave birth to their third child, Jane, in September 1868. Agnes, now eleven, was delighted, but having two infants to look after while her mother helped in the glassworks seemed to tire her. Joseph Junior was seven but refused to help and when their parents were not present, he could be rude and cruel to her. Agnes never complained, her stepmother always praised her, helped her with her schoolwork and had paid the wife of one of the men who worked in the factory to make Agnes two pretty dresses, one for Sabbath School and another to wear for outings to the park or when she visited friends.

Joseph was delighted when the *Sydney Morning Herald* ran a series of testimonials related to the Joseph Ross Perseverance Glass Bottle Works. The name had been chosen by Christina as her husband would never give up on his dream, she supported and encouraged his persistence. Perseverance was an appropriate name, as besides constant financial challenges in 1870, the glassworks was destroyed by fire. Being a high temperature fire-based process in a timber building the threat of fire was always present.

Christina had encouraged Joseph to take out some form of insurance as she realised the potential for financial ruination.

A number of businessmen had come together to form the Mutual Fire Insurance Association in 1841. They had created their own brigade by bringing two fire engines and two professional firefighters from England. Realising the potential losses, a number of insurance companies came together to form the Sydney Fire Establishment, also known as the Insurance Companies Fire Brigade. Three years later, Andrew Toring formed the Number 1 Volunteer Company, then helped to create several Volunteer Companies.

On the night of the fire, Christina with new-born baby Jane in her arms and the children, Agnes, twelve, Joseph, eight and Thomas, three, watched as horse-drawn fire engines arrived. The manually operated hand pumps were no match for the flames that leapt above the galvanised roof. Joseph and local men had grabbed buckets and formed a chain, hopelessly throwing the buckets' contents, just producing steam. Realising the building was lost, the men had turned their attention to prevent the flames from engulfing the heaps of coal that were essential to fuelling the furnaces. Christina was mesmerised by the crackle of flickering flames and the creak and groan of timbers contracting. Men yelled and cried for help, glass bottles shattering, then the roof caved in.

She watched the billowing plumes of black, sooty smoke that burnt her nose and throat. She was struck by the vivid glow and forced back by the blistering heat. As it was just past midnight, she knew that the factory would be empty except for the night watchman and she had seen him standing near Joseph, yelling instructions.

Again, Christina found it necessary to support and encourage Joseph. They had enough money to rebuild but had lost a large amount of stock and raw materials. Fortunately, their clients were supportive, many being co-dependent. Some of the larger companies placed large orders and prepaid to assure the glasswork's cash flow.

By the early 1870s, Joseph had made sufficient profits to purchase from Lattin's estate his share of the business. The factory was now located in Smith Street which ran between Camperdown Road and Park Street, one block south of Parramatta Road.

The influx of thousands of ex-gold miners into Sydney in the 1860s and 70s ushered in an era of growth and prosperity that was to transform Sydney from a struggling backwater town into an international city.

The replacement factory consisted of a series of weatherboard buildings with galvanised iron rooves. Inside one, a large brick furnace, conical in shape with high chimney punched through the roof. The furnace was heated by burning Newcastle coal at about five tons per week. There were two large crucibles to melt the basic ingredients of white sand from Surry Hills, lime produced from crushed shells, imported soda ash, and chemicals to colour the glass. The crucibles had to be heated for fourteen hours to melt the ingredients. Each could hold four hundred kilograms of molten glass, batches produced six times a week.

The factory made a range of bottles for chemists, bottles to hold sarsaparilla, wine, bitters, soda water and cordial. Another line of jars was for marmalade, jams, mustard and curry.

Joseph felt his hard work was paying off when he received a bronze medal for bottles he exhibited at the Intercolonial Exhibition in Sydney. Though not winning, the first two places were taken by bottles produced in Victoria, so he still promoted himself as the top NSW glass manufacturer. The General Industries and Arts exhibition was held in the Exhibition Building at Prince Alfred Park in Surrey Hills. The NSW Agricultural Society organised the exhibition to mark the centenary of Captain Cook's landing at Botany Bay. All Australian states and New Zealand had been invited to submit a display.

# Chapter 24

Though the business was going well, the family's personal life was shaken in October 1873 with the death of Agnes at their home in Smith Street, Camperdown. Her illness had been sudden and unexpected. She had been suffering from nausea, vomiting and a poor appetite. As a family, the Ross's were stoic. They had been taught to endure pain and hardship without showing their feelings or complaining. Agnes had initially experienced pain near her belly button which then moved to her right side. They had been dull pains that were irregular, however during the third night became severe. Agnes eventually had to tell her mother she had severe pain in her entire abdomen. She suddenly felt weak, and when Christina felt her forehead, she was burning up. Christina sent Joseph Junior to get his father and the doctor was called. His diagnosis was peritonitis, or burst appendix. He explained that there was little he could do, and Agnes died in the early hours of the morning. At only sixteen, she had become her mother's backstop. While her mother went to the factory early each morning to help stoke and light the furnaces, Agnes would get the breakfast for her siblings, do the washing, clean the house and prepare lunch. Christina would spend the afternoons tending to the children's education and together they would prepare the evening meal. When James had been born in 1870 and Elizabeth in 1872, Agnes had become their second mother.

The funeral was a simple family affair held at the local Balmain Cemetery. Christina could see, though already well used, the cemetery was relatively new. A meeting had been held of local residents in 1863 who sought to have their own cemetery in Balmain. This was a new residential estate that had only been laid out in 1852 but at the time things like access to parkland and cemeteries were less important than population density. The residents proposed establishing a fund to purchase land that could be used for community purposes. In the case of the cemetery, residents could subscribe for plots at one pound per plot, this to be matched by the government. Although a majority of the community were in favour, the plan was opposed by the developers, objecting on the grounds of hygiene and that it might impede future housing development and road construction. However, an act of Parliament in 1864 granted the community eleven acres, bounded by Norton and William Streets. The land was transferred to the Leichhardt Council in 1886 when a cemetery was established.

# Chapter 25

Joseph chose to move his operation from Smith Street, Camperdown to Australia Street, Camperdown. Christina and the family again had to pack up all their belongings and relocate, this time to 147 Denison Street which was behind the glassworks. The single-storey, semi-detached brick house of five rooms on a small block that had rear access from Denison Lane. At the time Joseph was twelve, Thomas, eight, Jane, six, James, four, and Elizabeth two. With Agnes gone, Christina had hired a housekeeper to help with the children but with five children aged twelve and under, each day was a challenge. This was added to by the fact she was heavily pregnant with her own sixth child.

Christina was also left to deal with Joseph's son Joseph, who liked to be called Joe and refused to answer to Joseph. He disliked his father and each time the two Josephs talked, it ended in an argument or worse, a physical altercation. Joe had become uncontrollable and was rarely at home. Christina had been told by a local police constable that the boy had been seen involved in a larrikin gang. Constable

Sullivan informed Christina that Joseph was part of the Orange Push Gang. This was one of a series of gangs, Orange Push being protestant, while the Rock Push were made up of Irish catholic youths. She had heard of them, everyone in Sydney knew to avoid the Rocks area. The Push gangs made life more unpleasant by stealing from and beating up pedestrians. The gangs had both boys and girls. Sullivan implied that some of the girls were worse than their male counterparts. They would prey on drunk seamen luring them into the dark alleys to be met, bashed and robbed by the gang. Sullivan laughed, 'Bit more than larrikins, they are supposed to be boisterous, badly behaved young men with an apparent disregard for convention, a maverick, these punks are just criminals.'

This didn't help Christina. The gangs were widely feared, rival gangs such as the Glebe Push, Miller's Point Push, Argyle Cut Push, Green Push, Orange Push, and the Forty Thieves, from Surry Hills, would often have territorial fights. Christina had read about a fight between the leader of the Orange Push, Sandy Ross, and the Catholic Green Push, Larry Foley. As legend had it, the bare-knuckle fight went for seventy-one rounds before police intervened. She was concerned about Sandy's surname, another Ross, not a known relative, but no one would know that. Foley was known as the best head puncher in Sydney. A sad claim to fame for a boy who was originally destined to become a priest but at eighteen ran off to Sydney to find work in construction. Foley met John "Black" Perry, a black Canadian, who had given him boxing lessons.

Christina struggled with mixed emotions. February was the joy for the birth of a healthy son, Francis, but only five months, later the death of their daughter Elizabeth. Her sweet little girl, only two years old. Elizabeth had developed a cold with blocked runny nose, and sneezing. It was July, the middle of winter, so colds were common and expected. On the third day she was suffering from a raised temperature and started to cough, especially at night. Over the next two days the cough became more frequent, and Elizabeth started to vomit after each attack. She had trouble eating and her breathing was laboured. When the doctor was called, he diagnosed whooping cough that had developed into pneumonia. He explained that about one in every two hundred babies who developed whooping cough died, sadly this was the case for Elizabeth. Her tiny body was buried in Balmain cemetery in 1874 next to Agnes' plot.

In addition to coping with loss, Christina was dealing with Joseph's anger and depression over the future of his business. Though it had done well, it was now suffering from a lack of skilled labour and also lack of sufficient credit.

Unfortunately, in August 1874, Joseph was again declared bankrupt. Though a great ideas man, Joseph constantly overextended himself thus Christina was forced to take on the financial control of the company with future liquid assets being in her name. The matter was cleared through the courts quickly and by September Joseph and his "J Ross" trademark was back in business again. This meant a change of suppliers as his largest creditor had been a local coal company.

# Chapter 26

Though she tried, Christina could not resolve the constant conflict between her husband and stepson Joe. Joe resented his father's authoritarian discipline, rebelling by refusing to work at the glass factory but also refusing to go to school. Joe had previously run away several times and his father had brought him before the police magistrate in an attempt to force him to change and attend school. During one of the occasions when Joe went missing, Joseph had placed an advertisement in the paper offering a reward for information about the location of his son, indicating he had breached the condition of his apprenticeship. This failed and not long after Joseph was brought before the court for ill-treating the boy.

When Joe was again brought before the court on 26 August 1873 under the Act for the Relief of Destitute Children his father refused to attend. Joe was charged with 'habitually wandering about the streets with no ostensible lawful occupation.' Christina attended the hearing indicating Joe was twelve years old, a protestant with some education at home but he would not stop at school and thus could neither read nor write and she had no control over him. Witnesses stated that Joe had been getting food at a King Street boarding house, telling them his father beat him and he was afraid to go home. Joe added that he had been away from home for several weeks and had been sleeping on some hay at the wharves.

The judge sentenced Joe to be placed on board the *Vernon* till his 16th birthday. In 1866, the Industrial Schools Act had been introduced to control "wayward children". This included children found wandering the streets, begging, abandoned or committing a crime. The act also allowed the government to declare any vessel or building to be a Public Institute School. Under the act, the former merchant sailing ship *Vernon* had been purchased in 1867. The ship was refitted under the guidelines of the Society for the Relief of Destitute Children, to provide a place of protection under good influences, to be trained in habits of honest industry. An all-boys institution initially moored off Garden Island in Sydney Harbour then moved in 1871 to be moored off Cockatoo Island. On board, the boys were given moral training, nautical and industrial training and elementary schooling. Joe was trained as a shoemaker. As with the other boys Joe had to tend the vegetable gardens on the island, with the island also used as a drill ground and recreational area.

When Joe arrived on the *Vernon* in 1873 it had recently had a new mate and eventual superintendent appointed. Frederick Neitenstein had a reputation as a reformer who believed in a combination of discipline, surveillance, physical drill and a system of grades. Joe again rebelled at this regimentation, so was often in conflict with authority. Joe's time on the *Vernon* did not seem to change him as he was again back in court in December 1880, aged 19, charged with larceny and sentenced to two months' imprisonment. In March 1882, he was again in court in the country town of Bathurst, NSW, charged with horse stealing and was sentenced to twelve months hard labour imprisonment. The family had little contact with him after this date but eventually, long after Joseph passed away, Joe is shown on the electoral rolls as a caretaker living at Woolooware Road, Burraneer Bay, and the home of his half-brother Thomas.

# Chapter 27

Always looking for new markets, Joseph was pleased to meet an acquaintance of Christina, Harriet Holtermann. The two women had been introduced while visiting a common friend. Over afternoon tea Christina had mentioned that her husband was a glass and bottle maker and Harriet discussed her husband Otto, who used bottles in his manufacturing and sale of a patent medicine called Holtermann's Life Preserving Drops. The women exchanged cards and a few weeks later the post contained an invitation for afternoon tea at the Holtermann's home in North Sydney.

Joseph hated the thought of having to get dressed in their best, to be sat in a usually hot and stuffy parlour, sipping tepid tea and listening to irrelevant social chat. Joseph actually preferred coffee, a taste he had developed while working in America. He had on one similar occasion asked the hostess if he could have coffee instead. The embarrassed woman had given him a filthy look, and Christina had berated him on the walk home for offending one of her friends. One good thing, these gatherings were normally over in about an hour but he knew that was a cost he was going to have to bear for a possible future market.

Christina had never visited the north shore. Though only a short ferry ride, she had not previously had a reason. One receipt of the invitation, Joseph had contacted friends to find out more about the Holtermanns. What he found was both fascinating and exciting. Though Otto was Prussian he had immigrated to Australia, via America, and made his money in mining. In 1882 at Hill End, the Star of Hope Mining Company, of which Otto was a partner, had discovered a considerable amount of gold including a nugget of ninety-three kilograms (three thousand troy ounces) worth around twelve thousand pounds. Otto had become an alderman on the Hill End Council in 1873 then moved to North Sydney where he became an alderman on the St Leonards Council in 1874. He had also been the licensee of the All Nations Hotel.

Once they alighted from the ferry, Christina and Joseph had taken a hansom cab to the address given. As the road leading to the residence climbed the hills above Lavender Bay, an enormous Italianate mansion came into view. It was immediately obvious why the invitation had called the house The Towers. The central tower was enormous, far beyond what would be expected for ornamentation, Christina thought it a conspicuous display. The decorative detail on the masonry walls and balustrades was unlike any she had seen in the colony as were the cast iron columns used on the veranda. The house was located in a truly picturesque spot that commanded extensive views.

On arrival, the Ross's were met by two couples. Harriet stepped forward and introduced her husband and then her sister Mary and husband Mr Ludwig Beyers. Greetings were formal, then Harriet led the party around a veranda to the rear of the home. Though there was a cool sea breeze, Joseph was pleased to find that tea was being served on a wide veranda, rather than a parlour or drawing room.

Mary chattered about Harriet meeting a young foreigner while they were living in the gold mining community of Hill End. Harriet had introduced his Polish friend and mining partner, Ludwig "Louis" Beyer to her and the two couples had a joint wedding. Harriet's expression told Christina that she was concerned that this level of intimate conversation on a first meeting was not appropriate. When Mary added that the men had made a fortune and moved to Sydney for their children to have better employment and marriage prospects, Harriet looked almost depressed, wondering what their guests would think of her and her chatty sister.

Harriet managed to redirect the conversation by stating that like Christina, Otto had a strong belief in supporting the community and had given sizeable donations to the Temperance League and to assist in establishing free local schools to support and encourage the less fortune within the community. This attempt to save face made Christina smile as she remembered Joseph remarking that one of Otto's businesses in Hill End had been as licensee of a hotel.

The three men stood silently taking in the view over the settlement of North Sydney, the harbour and its shipping and the southern shore with its coves and urban development.

Otto broke the prolonged silence,

'My wife told me you were a bottle maker, Mr Ross?'

Joseph chose to answer using his limited proficiency in German, which he had learnt while doing his journeyman year. 'I am interested in all types of glassmaking, I learnt my trade both in England and with Hans Siemens at his glassworks in Dresden.'

This surprised the other two, the tone of the conversation instantly changing. 'Perhaps, Mr Ross, you would like to see my workplace, we have some interesting experiments we have been doing?'

Christina was pleased for Joseph but realised that she was not included in the invitation, and though eager to see for herself, she would be left to endure the social conversation expected of her gender.

The men climbed the stairs of Otto's seventy-three-foot high masonry tower. At the top they were met by a fourth man, Charles Bayliss, who turned out to be Otto's technical assistant. While in Hills End,

Otto had met and travelled with photographer Henry Merlin and his young assistant, Charles. Henry and Otto shared the belief that photographs of this new world should be sent to Europe to encourage migrants. Otto had travelled with the two men taking photographs of most of New South Wales. When Merlin died in 1873, Otto wanted to complete the project with photos of Sydney itself.

At the top, a room was fitted with a hundred inch focal length lens used for photography. Joseph had never seen such precision glasswork. Otto indicated it had been specially imported from Germany. The northern wall was also unique as it consisted of a large construction designed to hold a sheet glass facing in a northerly direction. Otto explained that his assistant would coat a sheet of glass with an emulsion, the lens was uncapped for a set period of time resulting in the glass plate carrying a latent image. Charles would then place the glass in baths of chemicals. Charles laughed, adding the hardest part was carrying the plate of glass down the several flights of narrow stairs to allow it to be dried by an open fire. Otto showed Joseph two completed plates, one measuring four feet six inches by three feet two inches. The paper prints from the plates were breath-taking and Otto told Joseph of his plan to take them to the 1876 International Exhibition in Philadelphia and the 1878 Exposition Universelle Internationale in Paris. Joseph wished him well and assured him that his work was amazingly innovative. Otto's photographs were to win medals at both exhibitions.

After saying their farewells Joseph tried to describe to Christina what he had been shown but this only added to her frustration and anger at being excluded. The fact that Harriet mentioned she had never been allowed up the tower, as it was too dangerous for a woman, only made things sound worse.

Though Christina only met Harriet on a few further social occasions Joseph and Otto became close friends. Their bond was not so much photography as a shared interest in the rapid technological changes that were occurring in the colony. Both men were to exhibit at the 1879 Sydney International Exhibition with Holtermann being given a special bay in the Garden Palace.

Joseph had found that Otto's election to the New South Wales Legislative Assembly for the seat of St Leonards in 1882 would open more doors for him to government figures and future contacts.

Sadly, Otto died on his forty-seventh birthday in 1885. Eventually the Holtermann house would become one of the boarding houses at the Sydney Church of England Grammar School, known as Shore.

# Chapter 28

Disaster struck again on 17th October 1876 when fire destroyed the Australia Street factory. At four a.m., fire broke out in the pot room with the Newtown and Camperdown Volunteer Fire Brigades plus the Number 3 Volunteer Fire Company attending. Fire spread rapidly through the buildings with tools and stock destroyed. Damage amounted to one thousand five hundred pounds sterling but insurance only covered eight hundred pounds sterling. Regardless, the decision was made to rebuild.

Prior to the fire, the glass factory had been receiving nuisance complaints from neighbours about noise and dust. The firemen who attended the scene went so far as to say the fire could have been caused by an act of vandalism. There was no blame directed towards the Ross's. It was obvious to all they had not gained in any way from the fire. One of the exterior doors had been forced and the night watchman indicated he had seen some youths wandering along the street earlier that evening.

Christina was aware of local concern. Several women had made comments to her when she was shopping at the local markets. There had also been letters, that Joseph had ignored, and when Christina had purchased a house in a local street the owner made it clear he was glad to get away from the growing number of industries and the associated pollution they were creating. This had not worried Christina at the time. She had offered him less than he asked and really didn't care why he was selling, the house was a good investment, adding to the two others she had already purchased. This property she registered in the name James Ross, her son who was six at the time.

Realising the need to try and keep the local community on side, and not risk the problem their earlier factory had faced in Balmain, Christina recommended that Joseph place advertisements in local papers encouraging people to visit the factory site with any concerns, issues and recommendations. The advertisements referred to the business as a "most valuable and important one in the colony."

Though a few people came to look at the plans, most were just interested in seeing the damage done by the fire. With no written complaints Joseph built a new factory of brick with shingle roof, the new business considered safer in terms of flammability.

Business again thrived and as other industries established and expanded the demand for bottles exploded. However, on 28th February 1878, another fire started when a lamp left burning in Joseph's office set the timber walls ablaze. The alarm was raised with both local and city fire brigades quickly arriving at the scene. Though the fire was contained to the main factory area, the Standard Insurance Company would only pay for half of the damage, as they felt Joseph was partially culpable, the loss estimated at over two thousand pounds sterling. As with previous setbacks, Christina took on the role of encourager, both with Joseph and glassworks employees. She felt the need to meet with the journeymen assuring them that the business would be back to work quickly, their continued support essential. She called in each of the boys, giving each a coin, a small bonus, paying for their loyalty.

The tactic worked and all returned once the factory was repaired. With renewed enthusiasm the business again continued to grow and at the Sydney Garden Palace Exhibition of 1879 Joseph received the highest award of merit, an official recognition that his bottles were equal to the quality of overseas imports.

# Chapter 29

During the 1870s, Joseph's glass factory acted almost as a monopoly. However, by the early 1880s local competition increased and thus the wholesale prices of bottles dropped by fifty percent. Companies such as Co-operative Flint Glass Co. in Abattoir Road, Balmain used overseas trained workers to produce a similar product. At the time, consumption in NSW stood at twenty-nine million bottles annually.

There was also competition developing in other colonies such as Victoria where a glass company was founded by the chemists Alfred Felton and Frederick Grimwade, who set up a small furnace at Port Melbourne with British glassblowers in 1867. The company was called the Melbourne Glass Bottle Works Company in 1872; it expanded to Sydney in 1903.

Joseph introduced new technology especially in terms of the types of melting crucibles he used. He was able to increase his production threefold allowing his market to expand to most major towns in NSW as well as interstate.

Changes in technology were necessary as the colony of NSW had become a free market for all types of goods, and in Joseph's case cheap glassware from Belgium and Germany. As a result, Joseph had cut his staff from seventy-five men and boys to around twenty-five. He resorted to spending more time himself working on the factory floor and to the use of mainly foreign skilled journeymen, who worked as required to fill orders and worked at several different companies. These men insisted on being paid in cash on the day they worked thus prepayment of orders was increasingly important to keep cash flowing. To cut overheads, Christina again became more hands-on, taking over the role of the pre-dawn lighting of the furnaces to ensure they were ready when the men arrived. Another cost saving strategy was the reduction in the number of permanent employees that were apprenticed. A new category of workers, improvers, were introduced, with them picking up skills informally, on the job. The children Thomas, Jane and Frank were required to spend several hours each day helping their mother to clean, sweep floors, shovel coke into the furnace, and the boys were also required to feed and brush the horses.

It was not till the 1880 Public Institution Act that schooling was made compulsory for the first time. The act required attendance of more than one hundred and forty days per year, this left plenty of time for children to still work in both paid and unpaid employment.

The act also removed all state aid for church schools and established a Department of Public Education. The Protestant church agreed in the interest of common benefit for children, but the Catholic Church rejected the concept and declared all public schools as irreligious. This was leading to a greater religious and cultural divide.

During this period, 1878–1888, while physically supporting Joseph in the factory, Christina was to have six additional children, and faced the challenges and trials associated with them. John Donald was born 1878 but died a few days after birth; John was born 1880; Josephine Barbara Sinclair born 1882; Alexander born 1884; Elijah born 1886 but he was a sickly child and died aged seven months, and Edith Mary born 1888 who died 1889, aged seventeen months. At the time of Edith's birth, Christina's thirteenth child, Christina was aged forty-two and Joseph fifty-three.

# Chapter 30

In 1882, their company was called the Australian Glass Bottle Works and advertised as specialising in bottles.

The development of carbonated drinks stimulated the change in bottle design. The Codd bottle was developed to maintain pressure within the bottle, a glass ball often referred to as a marble was introduced to cap the bottle as the pressure against the marble blocked the rim to prevent the escape of gas.

December 1882 saw the glassworks being indicted for smoke nuisance. The case was held in April 1883 with witnesses referring to dense and foul, sulphur-smelling smoke coming from the factory's two large and four small chimneys. The neighbours complained of chest pain, soot falling on their washing and covering their homes, a coach painter complained it threatened his business. Joseph's was not the only business in the case as Robert Fowler Pottery was located in the same street and also had larger chimneys. The Camperdown council was aware of how important these industries were to the local community, especially in terms of employment, thus within a few weeks Joseph was found not guilty, and he was discharged.

Christina again accessed the press and penned a letter to the *Evening News.* It indicated that the Ross works were of public benefit and employed a large amount of labour and provided a local industry that otherwise the colonies would have to rely on imports from Europe for. The letter went on to explain that this would result in much higher prices for bottles. It also indicated that bottles from other colonies such as Victoria would cost twice as much. This was one in a series she penned, her nom de plumes or pseudonyms taken from surnames she had read in the Sydney paper.

# Chapter 31

While Joseph was busy working with the protectionist movement, Christina attended a meeting at which Mr Eli Johnson, a visiting American temperance lecturer was presenting. Though this fitted with her childhood beliefs, her interests were aroused by information given related to the formation of the Sydney Woman's Christian Temperance Union (WCTU). As with the movements her father had been part of in Scotland, this new union was primarily dedicated to the total abstinence from alcohol and other harmful drugs. All the members signed a pledge and were encouraged to get their families to do the same. Christina knew Joseph would be supportive but because of his business ventures and inclination to a casual drink, would not sign.

Christina saw the WCTU aims in a broader context, she equated temperance with the welfare of women and children and saw the potential of the union as a lobby group. She noted with interest a section in Johnson's lecture that referenced an American sister organisation that focussed on a campaign for women's suffrage.

Besides these broader goals, the Temperance Union had adopted some hands-on strategies, the first, a petition against the new Licensing Bill that was before the Colonial Parliament. Christina spoke against the second, planned protests against the employment of women as barmaids in hotels. Christina knew several women who worked in this role. They were hard working, supporting families like her own. She questioned why it was the women who should be punished because of the behaviour of their predominantly male clientele. After all, the union advocated 'an equal moral standard for men and women.' To Christina, this meant equal rights, including in employment. No one was going to tell her she could not work next to men in the factory, or own property in her own name. She understood that the organisation was conservative by nature, promoting traditional home values and the role of women. Many like her, saw the opportunity for a more progressive focus. However, she could see in the faces of some of the other women, questions related to her motives. After all, she was a bottle maker's wife.

Starting on a small scale, the union was strongly influenced in 1885 by the visit of Mary Leavitt, the first world missionary of the American Union. She encouraged the growth of additional unions in the colonies of Queensland, South Australia and Tasmania. Besides attending her lecture in Sydney

Christina had met Mary during an afternoon tea at a friend's home. She was amazed at the strength and determination of this woman. Mary talked openly about her life, her marriage and divorce after having three daughters. She had then been forced to establish her own independent life, setting up her own private school in Boston, Massachusetts. It had been a success and at one time had sixty-five students, two full time teachers, and four specialist language teachers, with Mary teaching the French and Latin classes. In 1881, she handed over the reins of her school and began working full-time for the Woman's Christian Temperance Union. Christina had thought that one day she might like to open her own school, but with the demands of her children and the level of reliance Joseph had on her, it was an unlikely scenario.

Mary explained that her world mission had actually got off to a poor start. The WCTU had failed to fund her as hoped, thus she had left America with only thirty-five dollars from her own funds. The union had also declined to issue a formal letter of introduction, thus she relied on a recommendation from her own congregational minister. On her way to Australia, she had first held a series of lectures in the Sandwich Islands (Hawaiian Islands) where she had to use interpreters to speak to the indigenous Hawaiians, Portuguese and Japanese audiences. She felt blessed that the ladies of the newly formed

Honolulu WCTU had given her four hundred dollars towards the next leg of her world mission. She used some of this to board the Pacific Mail steamship, the S.S. *Zealandia*, travelling as a steerage passenger. Over the next seven months in New Zealand she visited towns, large and small, on both islands. She started to set up unions, these later being taken up by a local suffragist, Anne Ward, who created a national organisation.

It was after her arrival in mid-August 1885 that Christina had met her. Wishing to help, Christina accompanied her to meetings in Newtown, and Lithgow. The latter, the furthest Christina had been from the harbour city since her arrival. She felt great excitement as their small party boarded the steam train heading through Parramatta over the Nepean River then slowly up the grades of the Blue Mountains. Joseph had told her that the last section of the line had only been opened in 1869, what he described as an amazing feat. He referred to zigzags and viaducts, to allow the train to climb the steep mountain slopes. Christina thought the seven-span sandstone viaduct near the eastern base of the mountain, at a place called Knapsack, particularly impressive. The descent on the western side was equally fascinating with deep rock cuttings, three viaducts with semi-circular arches and a short tunnel. When they disembarked at Lithgow their train was steaming on to a town called Bathurst.

Though they were received well by the women within the Lithgow community, a mixture of shop owner's wives, copper and coal miner wives and some pastoralist's wives, the town's male leaders were noticeable by their absence. They were hosted to a fine lunch by a Mrs Brown, the wife of a Scottish Presbyterian farmer, at their home called Eskbank House. Brown had been a flour miller but made most of his money as a mine owner. The women were impressed by the views over the Lithgow Valley which could be seen while standing in the extensive ornamental gardens. The house, a single-storey Victorian Georgian-style residence had been constructed of local sandstone in the 1840s. Three sides of the house were surrounded by a stone-flagged veranda.

Christina would have dearly loved to join Mary on her tour through Queensland and Tasmania but knew that was not viable. While in Australia, Mary founded five branches of the WCTU in Queensland, three in Tasmania and one in New South Wales and South Australia. Though pregnant with her twelfth child, Elijah, Christina stood for hours watching the departure of the ship that was carrying Mary to Japan in April 1886. Christina felt she had a strong bond with this like-minded soul and the two corresponded while she continued her mission in Japan, Korea and China. After China, Mary presented lectures in Thailand, Singapore and Burma, followed by a year in India. After India she toured Africa, finally arriving in Britain in 1889.

Christina loved Mary's letters, full of descriptive language, and social comment. She would take them to meetings to share with her fellow members. Mary's mission continued through Europe in 1890, then in 1891, Egypt, Turkey Israel and Syria. In 1892, the letters were addressed from South America, Argentina, Uruguay and Brazil. Christina became worried for Mary's safety as one letter explained she had suffered with yellow fever, malaria and in Brazil men from a college had thrown paving stones at her while she was speaking.

Christina had drawn a large map of the world on which she marked Mary's travels, most of the places, she and her friends had never heard of. In one of the last letters during her mission, Mary calculated she had visited over forty-three countries, travelled around one hundred thousand miles and held one thousand six hundred meetings. She had crossed the equator eight times and used the services of two hundred and ninety different interpreters in forty-seven languages. Mary also wrote to Christina about her other causes. She questioned the need for continued British rule of India, and capital punishment for women. Christina considered her as one of, if not the best, role model for women. A person with convictions, willing to give her life in support of her beliefs.

Further growth of the WCTU would occur in 1889 with the visit of the American Union's second missionary, Jessie Ackerman. She had a stronger focus on women's suffrage, the area that was becoming Christina's major interest. Christina believed that true economic power was helped by those who could vote and thus make laws. She wanted the right to vote and was an advocate for equal pay. Though she hadn't discussed this with Joseph, she knew he would support the first but would argue against the second.

In 1889, Rose Scott and Mary Windeyer had helped set up the Women's Literacy Society in Sydney, which grew into the Womanhood Suffrage League of New South Wales. Where she could, Christina supported both physically and financially the work of Scott who wrote, debated, lectured and argued until in 1902 the Women's Suffrage Act became law in New South Wales. Christina helped lobby for the establishment of Children's Courts for juvenile offenders and for the age of consent to be raised. Another focus area for their group was the call for a more comprehensive and equitable system of family maintenance to be established.

Christina's experience with the NSW courts had been limited to attending, in lieu of Joseph, court actions related to his son Joe. On these occasions she saw first-hand how Joe was treated as an object, with no real consideration of a child's uniqueness and differences.

Christina was already a member of a colonial Women's Franchise League. This had been formed in the colonies mimicking the British organisation created by the suffragette Emmeline Pankhurst together with her husband Richard in 1889. The colony's action group aimed to secure the vote for both married and single women in local elections. Christina was very familiar with the power and influence of local councillors and felt that many of the local women who she called friends, and like her owned property or business, could and would do the job better.

Her group was inspired by success in the colony of South Australia. Women in that colony achieved the right to vote in 1894 and stand for office in 1895 following the world's first Constitutional Amendment (Adult Suffrage) Act in 1894. The argument had been put to her that this was due to the fact that South Australia had been established as a free settlement, no convicts. She could see how this difference might slow the granting of rights in NSW as the social divide between free settlers and convict stock was still wide.

# Chapter 32

Joseph realised that the colony's free trade policy was resulting in loss of business to cheaper Belgian and German glassware. In 1852, the NSW Parliament had passed the Deas-Thompson Tariff named after the then colonial secretary of NSW. This restricted the articles to which a tariff would apply. These included beer and spirits, tobacco and tobacco products, sugar and sugar products like molasses, tea and coffee.

Joseph was an inaugural committee member of the Chamber of Manufacturing NSW that followed from the 1826 Sydney Chamber of Commerce. The first meeting of the Chamber of Manufacturing was held at Sydney Town Hall where the rules and regulations were adopted, and Archibald Forsyth was elected the first president. The chamber focused most of its efforts on policy lobbying, setting up a Protection Union in direct opposition to the Free Traders led by Sir Henry Parkes who had been five times the premier of the colony. Parkes was a disciple of Richard Cobden, an English radical, Liberal and campaigner for free trade, who was associated with the Anti-Corn Law League. This political movement in Great Britain aimed at abolishing the law that protected landowner's interest, a levee on imported wheat, forcing the price of bread to rise. However, at a meeting at Hotel Australia the chamber abandoned the idea of political lobbying and adopted a position of non-political lobbying. Their concern was both the competition from overseas manufacturers but also from the colony of Victoria with its protectionist policies.

Joseph was concerned that the Victorian colony had adopted a very different approach to protection of industry. It had developed a very strong protectionist sentiment to the business community. The movement was led by David Syme, who had assumed the editorship of The Age newspaper in Melbourne in 1850. His vision and thus the focal point of the paper was of a self-sufficiency for the colony to be achieved through restrictive tariffs. The Age was used repeatedly to enforce a gradual increase in protectionism to prevent any reduction in tariffs.

Joseph decided that the NSW colony needed something similar thus set about creating his own newspaper.

Though Joseph was very strong in his opinions he was happy to take a back seat to a young activist who made his leadership aspirations very clear from the first meeting. Though twenty-six years his junior, John Farleigh was impressive. Joseph had met his father Edward who had arrived in the colonies from County Sligo, Ireland, the same year as himself and had established a tannery at Canterbury. Joseph admired the company name, King of Mimosa Leather, and had visited their boot upper factory in Kent Street, Sydney. In 1901 the company would take on a new trademark: Australian Leather.

Joseph could see a lot in common between John Farleigh and his own son Thomas. Both young men were ambitious, both adopting a managerial approach to their respective father's businesses without being hands on. Both were focussed on the business accounts and management and had aspirations re local and state government positions. Not surprising when Joseph encouraged Thomas to attend a meeting of the Australian Chamber of Manufacturing, though Thomas was twenty and John twenty-four, the two men formed an immediate friendship.

They both were great believers in the application of scientific research to industry and the importance of training their workers. This was harder for Thomas as Joseph was a craftsman discouraging mechanisation and insisting on the use of journeymen, like himself, specialist workers, who were task orientated as they were paid based on their team's daily output.

Though Joseph was supportive of Thomas's new friends, Christina had concerns. It was obvious to her that he was dissatisfied with his current life. Where her other sons worked long hours, often late into the night, Thomas considered himself management. He would often leave early, especially on Fridays and wouldn't return till late Sunday. He was often seen at the theatre at King and York Streets, Sydney, for performances of the New Tivoli Minstrel and Grand Speciality Company of Forty Artists, a vaudeville show managed by a London—born comedian and entrepreneur Harry Richards. In 1893 this had relocated to the old Garrick Theatre that was renamed the Tivoli. Thomas laughed at the topical songs, often aimed at local politicians, bawdy sketches, but most of all the chorus line of gorgeously and scantily clad young women. He didn't care what his family would think, he didn't have their puritan leanings. One of his favourite performers was Lottie Collins and her song "Ta-ra-ra Boom-de-ay".

When not in the theatre he would meet his friends in the Grand Central Coffee Place in the adjoining Imperial Arcade. The arcade stretched from Pitt to Castlereagh Street. Another favoured area within the complex was the Imperial Arcade Hotel and in its dining room Thomas could enjoy a seven-course lunch for two shillings, promoted as the "best served luncheon in the city." The arcade was an impressive structure, seven floors, protruding galleries, cedar staircases, tiled floors, cast iron balusters and timber framed shop fronts. When it opened it was considered the very latest in shopping centres with 38 boutiques selling fashionable clothing and accessories. Its basement offered a range of cafes and hotel space was located on the upper floors. On several occasions he used rooms in the hotel to host private parties of close friends and ladies from the theatre. It is at these he gained the taste for strong alcoholic beverages, if it was there he would try it.

For a change, his group would visit either the Gaiety Theatre in Castlereagh Street (originally the Catholic Guild Hall) where the London Comedy Company assured an evening of belly laughs, or the Theatre Royal also in Castlereagh Street between King and Rowe Streets. This theatre was led by J.C. Williamson and tended to offer musical comedy and straight plays.

The Royal Strand, also known as the Royal Foresters' Hall, was another venue but not for theatre. This is where Thomas went to gamble on boxing. Not a theatre, but a place where he felt relaxed was the Royal Exchange Hotel. The publican, Duncan McPherson had become a close friend and though he had been fined when caught diluting Wolfe Schnapps with soda water and a cheap local gin, Duncan was a bit of a soul mate. Billiards was their shared distraction and the Royal Exchange had one of the best billiard saloons in the city.

Thomas also enjoyed the thrills of the circus. At that time, the Wirth Brothers Circus was the largest, and he remembered having to see it in Newtown, a walk from home but at that stage the outskirts of the city. This was because those who he called The Nobs, had petitioned the city mayor over the noise and traffic that the circus would generate. At sixpence a head entry, Thomas was impressed by the show and not surprised when the circus left Australia in 1893 for a seven-year-long world tour. Run by four brothers, each seemed to be doing everything, each man a musician, tumbler, club-swinger and trapeze artist.

One memorable circus evening for Thomas was when he was invited to a performance by the Fitzgerald Brothers Circus as his friends had been informed that there was to be a royal visitor. There with his retinue was the twenty-nine-year-old heir to the Austro-Hungarian throne, His Imperial and Royal Highness, archduke of Austria, Franz Ferdinand d'Este, who had arrived in Sydney aboard the SMS *Kaiserin Elizabeth*, a cruiser of the Austro-Hungarian navy during a world tour. Thomas spoke to some of his party and was informed that they were on a private visit and going to a place called Nyngan for some outback hunting of exotic animals.

Thomas was both amused and offended when reading the account of the Archduke's visit. He had been accompanied by his personal taxidermist, three counts, a major-general, a zoologist from Vienna and the NSW minister for public institutions. They travelled on a special train to Narromine, four hundred and fifty kilometres west of Sydney and by lunch on the first day the archduke had shot five kangaroos. After a barbeque of lamb chops and a bottle of hock, he shot pelican, brolgas, eagles and parrots. Over the next few days, he shot bush turkey, emu and two black swans, a few koalas and possum. Getting back to Sydney he attended High Mass at St Mary's Cathedral, did a quick inspection of a meat works then headed to the Wollondilly River. This was his most wanted kill, a scientific fascination, a platypus. Critics stated the archduke loved a good slaughter and during his lifetime would go on to kill over three hundred thousand animals. In years to come, Thomas, unlike most who read the newspaper found one headline humorous. The archduke had been shot, assassinated in 1914. For the world it would be the commencement of World War One, for Thomas it was nature's revenge for the innocent platypus.

# Chapter 33

Christina accompanied Joseph when he was brought before a parliamentary select committee, established by free traders to enquire into allegations that protectionist Ninian Melville had corruptly helped Ross to sell land at Newtown to the Department of Railways at an inflated valuation. Ninian was accused of accepting twenty-five pounds from "a bottle manufacturer" but claimed it was simply a man paying him a debt he owed. Fortunately for Joseph the committee found the charge "not proven." This caused angst in both the political and business community about the value and honesty of select committees.

Ninian Melville, Joseph's co-conspirator, had been a Scottish cabinet maker, the son of a convict transported to the colony for stealing clothing. Ninian had set up a furniture making business in Sydney, but it failed in 1866 due to cheaper and better-quality foreign imports. He moved to Melbourne, becoming an undertaker but had returned to Sydney in 1874. He established an undertaking business in Newtown where he and Joseph had become friends due to their shared belief in protectionism. The two often met to plan their campaign hoping to increase the degree of protection industries could achieve in the NSW colony. Victoria had adopted a protectionist platform, but the political leader of New South Wales favoured free trade. Joseph also found him a useful contact in that Ninian was active in local politics, spending time as a member of the Newtown Council and was elected mayor in 1882. Though he was elected to the NSW Legislative Assembly in 1880, having Ninian as an ally did nothing for Joseph's own reputation. Like several of his previous business associates, Christina had counselled Joseph about the importance of community opinion. When it came to business contacts Joseph seemed to walk around wearing blinkers, blind to these men's faults.

Ninian had been described as a colourful character and had already faced unproven allegations of bribery. The premier, Sir Henry Parkes, had gone so far as to describe him as 'the veriest charlatan that ever lived.' Ninian had also rated a mention in a poem by the author and bush poet Henry Kendall. In 1880 Kendell released his third collection of poetry called *Songs from the Mountains*. One satirical poem was entitled "The song of Ninian Melville." However, immediately after publication the poem was considered possibly libellous, and though the book had already sold two hundred and fifty copies it was recalled. The poem was replaced by "Christmas Creek" and the book republished in 1881.

The poem did get an airing in the NSW Parliament in April 1887 when a member speaking against Melville quoted the last verse, under parliamentary privilege, noting that Kendell was dead and thus not liable to action against him. The verse begins referring to a parliament with high august traditions, lordly words, halls familiar to our fathers, that in past days was exalted. However, it concludes with:

> "We in ash, we in sackcloth, sorry for the insults cast,
> By a crowd on bitter boobies, on the grandeur of the past,
> Take away your penny whistles, boy, it is no good to me,
> Last invention is a bladder with the title of M.P."

Kendall had also accused Ninian of making a name for himself by attacking formal religion. Though a member of the Primitive Methodist community and also a member of a temperance order, "Ninny" as he was known, with his large pipe and long black coat and topper had often been seen in public houses telling surprisingly bold stories that often showed an imprudent lack of respect. Kendall called him out for not practicing what he preached.

Initially Christina, during Ninian's visits to their home both socially and in his role with the protectionist movement, had on the surface found him to be a straight talker. She had admired his demands for sabbatarian and temperance legislation. Throughout her own life she had held the strong belief that as a Christian there needed to be the upholding of Sunday as God's Day. Like Christina, Ninian was a member of the Independent Order of Rechabites also known as the Sons and Daughters of Rechab. This group had initially attracted Christina as it focussed not just on encouraging abstinence, but its members provided assistance during time of sickness, death and hardship. As a voluntary association their focus was on mutual aid through trying to assist the local unemployed in areas such as gaining medical access and encouraging education. However, Christina soon began to realise that the man was superficial, all show, no real conviction.

# Chapter 34

In early 1886, Christina's second surviving child, daughter Jane Ross, married Richard Jones in Newtown. Richard had been born in Warrington, Lancashire, becoming a builder after immigrating to Sydney. Though in some ways dysfunctional, the Ross family were close, and this outsider didn't fit in. Christina had expected them to move into one of the five semi-detached houses she currently owned in Bray Street, but Richard made it clear he was his own man and not interested in being part of the Ross glass business.

Christina had come to rely on Jane to help with the younger children while she worked alongside Joseph in the factory. At the time of Jane's marriage, Christina had just given birth to Elijah and still had Alexander aged two, Josephine aged four, John aged six and Frank aged twelve to care for and educate.

When Elijah died on the 30th April 1887, aged seven months, Christina partly blamed Jane, as though Christina's housekeeper helped look after the children, when Elijah became ill, unspoken sentiments considered that he would have been all right if Jane was still there.

In 1888 Jane gave birth to a son, Richard James Jones. A second child, daughter Edith Christina Jones was born 1891. A third, a son Jessie Frazer Jones born 1892, then in 1894, the birth of daughter Josephine Viney Jones.

In April 1897, Jane died at Potts Point aged twenty-nine. The family were living at the time at 108 Alice Street, Newtown. Separate funeral notices appeared from Mr Richard Jones; Mr and Mrs Joseph Ross, Messrs Thomas and Frank Ross (of Ross Brothers, bottle makers, Erskineville); Mr and Mrs James Boag; Joseph, John, Alexander and Josephine Ross; Mr and Mrs Thomas Ross (uncle).

However, the ongoing rift between Christina and her daughter's husband could be seen when the Jones children were placed by their father in the Randwick Asylum for Destitute Children where they remained till June 1901 after Richard remarried in May of that year. The asylum was run by the Society for the Relief of Destitute Children and housed up to eight hundred children at a time in large dormitories, often called barracks. The NSW government funded the institution till 1888 from then the society had to rely on donations. Most of the children were between three and ten and because they had one or both parents were not eligible for admission to a government run Orphan School. Every child admitted by their parent was to remain until the age of nineteen or, in the case of females when they married before that age. However as in the case of Jane's children, parents could reclaim their children at any time.

Though Christina had lost children, Elijah in 1887 and Edith Mary, born 1888 died 1889, at the time of Jane's death Christina's youngest, Alexander, aged fourteen, was working in the glassworks. Those who knew the fate of the Jones children questioned the actions and motives of their grandmother Christina. From the outside they saw a wealthy woman, owner of several homes in which she had tenants, living in a large house with a housekeeper. They wondered why the Ross family couldn't have done more to help and protect the Jones children. People knew that for children in this type of institution life was described as monotonous and reliant on routine and discipline. As the Jones children entered the institution aged nine, six, five and three, they were given a basic education from teachers who were from the state's Council of Education. At twelve, many of the children would be given apprenticeships learning a trade but only Richard Junior had reached that age while in the asylum.

Another risk facing the children in the asylum was epidemic diseases, with such large numbers massed together. There had been such an outbreak in 1867 when seventy-seven children died from whooping cough. In 1873 the Royal Commission into

Public Charities, led by Justice William Windeyer had criticised the Randwick asylum. Reformers were concerned that such a place neglected the needs of children implying they were condemned to dehumanisation. In 1881, the State Children Relief Act created the State Children's Relief Board to remove any child under twelve and place them in boarding-out home care. However, for some children such as the Jones' the asylum was seen as temporary care, and as long as a parent retained influence and kept visiting rights they remained at the asylum. As a result, the Randwick Asylum remained open till 1914 when the Commonwealth Government during World War One took over the buildings as a military hospital. In April 1915, the last of the children were removed. Records show that over the years the asylum functioned, two hundred and seventeen children died on site, many buried in unmarked graves on the grounds.

The Jones children were never spoken about in the Ross home. Joseph chose to ignore the situation and when Frank and John asked their mother about their nieces and nephews they got a curt, 'that's their father's problem, don't mention them again.' Both boys were old enough to realise that this was a harsh reaction by a hard women, opting now to distance themselves a little more from their mother.

# Chapter 35

On the 15th of December 1886, Christina's son James Ross died aged sixteen. He was courageous, dauntless and definitely a little daring. Being naturally curious he sometime overstepped the boundaries set both his parents, and society, but was always willing to face the outcomes of his decisions and actions. Physically he was taller than his siblings, but with the same masses of curly hair and blue eyes. His hard muscular physique attributed him a greater social status among his peers. This naturally attracted girls and unbeknown to his mother, James was thought by many to be a bit of a Casanova. Christina would refer to him as 'her larrikin', but in a positive way, good-hearted but with a careless disregard for social norms and expectations. Of all her children he made her laugh, he had a natural cuteness, endearing with his apparent innocence and exuberance. Her memories of her precious son were often focussed on him standing next to her, both covered in soot as they shovelled coal into the furnace, James white teeth gleaming as he held up a lump of coal, 'look this one looks like and elephant'.

James died at his parents' home, the residence of the glass works, Australia Street, Camperdown following a horse-riding accident. Besides learning the art of glass blowing, James's love of animals meant he had pleaded his father to put him in charge of the horses used to pull the large wagon that carried the finished bottles to the port or other factories. The wagon had been purchased for two hundred pounds from George T. Bennett's Wagon Works at St Marys. Bennett's made the largest wagons in the Southern Hemisphere, which he painted either green and red or red and blue, like the one the Ross's purchased. Bennett often gave these enormous wagons nicknames such as The Maxina, King of the Road and The Pioneer. Joseph had gone to inspect Bennett's factory prior to the purchase of a new wagon for Ross Brothers and had been hosted at the Bennett's home called Bronte House, a fine Victorian Gothic/Italianate mansion.

At night, the four Clydesdale horses were kept in a barn behind the factory but when not in use were cared for by a boy, Harry, employed for that specific purpose. Under James' supervision, Harry would feed and groom the horses and during the days lead them to Victoria Park to graze. The park had originally been part of Grose Farm that in 1853 had been designated as the site for the University of Sydney. Cattle and horses grazed freely on the land but when that was not available the Cleveland Paddocks, an area that became Prince Alfred Park, was used as it was public reserve. The park's name had been changed in 1867 to honour Prince Alfred, second eldest son of Queen Victoria. The prince was the first member of the royal family to visit Australia and had attracted large crowds. He was on a world tour on the steam frigate HMS *Galatea*. On the 12th of March, an Irish produce merchant, Henry O'Farrell, shot at and wounded Price Alfred at Clontarf where he was attending a picnic organised as a fundraiser for the Sydney Sailors' Home. The shooting increased the tension between the Irish Catholics and English, the incident being labelled "Fenian terrorism." The following day a meeting was held in Sydney with nearly twenty-thousand people gathering in protest. The local newspapers had fanned public indignation.

James had heard of the incident, but like most youths his age, thought little about it. James also had his own horse, a spirited gelding that he used to lead two of the Clydesdales while Harry had to walk leading the others. It was on one of these days in Prince Alfred Park that James encouraged his horse to jump a fallen tree. The horse clipped its fore legs, throwing James, who landed against the tree's trunk. There were no obvious signs of an injury, just a trickle of blood running from his nose and out of his left eye. James tried to stand but vomited and collapsed. Harry tied the four dray horses to the tree and lifted James back onto his horse, leading it back to the glassworks.

Though a doctor was called, James did not regain consciousness and died that evening. The newspaper referred to a Presbyterian burial, a nine by seven plot buried by Melville and Son, undertakers. It noted that James was buried near his half-sister Agnes Ross. For Christina the loss was almost intolerable, James had been as much a friend as a son. Not getting to say goodbye and tell him how much she had loved and admired him was taken from her. She regretted that the public demonstration of emotion, even the simple act of the words, was something that her family seemed to be repressed in.

# Chapter 36

In 1887, Joseph was the founding director of the Australian Newspaper Co. Ltd which launched the protectionist newspaper the *Australian Star*. The paper was a daily English paper first published Thursday 1st of December 1887 by Arthur Smyth at its offices at 78 King Street, Sydney. The paper was sold for one penny. The founding editor was W. H. Traill, a strong protectionist who later represented the electorate of South Sydney in the NSW Legislative Assembly. The *Star* would become *The Sun* in 1910.

Joseph liked Traill's attitudes and writing style. Joseph knew little about newspapers and publishing, but Traill had the experience to allow this fledgling paper to succeed. In 1869, Traill was working on the staff of the *Brisbane Courier* when he purchased the *Darling Downs Gazette*. In 1873 to 1878 he had served as editor of *The Queenslander* but moved his family to Sydney becoming the editor of *The Sydney Mail*.

Traill, being a protectionist, saw the venture being proposed by Joseph as a new opportunity. He, like Joseph, was a member of the newly formed

Protectionist or Liberal Party that advocated protective tariffs. The new *Australian Star* would be an essential voice for their party. Joseph asked Christina to help him write articles with particular reference to glass manufacturing. Though they would appear in the paper accredited to Joseph, she took pride in seeing her words in print. Readers found her writing style clear and concise with several of Joseph's business acquaintances requesting that he write similar articles about their own businesses. Christina enjoyed reading the rough drafts and technical information these men would send to Joseph. It was in connection with these that she decided to reach out to Thomas for help. They opted for the Café Francaise as the place they would meet, at a back table Thomas would read and make notes on her articles. Though Christina asked after the girls, Isabel was never mentioned.

Joseph was disappointed when told that Traill, after less than a year with the *Star*, was leaving as he had purchased *The Bulletin*. The Bulletin was a magazine first published in Sydney in 1880 by its founders J. F. Archibald and John Haynes. Joseph knew that Traill was a regular contributor to the magazine but didn't consider it a threat to his own paper, The Bulletin being more about sensationalised news rather than serious political commentary. In spite of this, both Joseph and Christina read and enjoyed the magazine with its strong nationalist sentiments. Its writers and cartoonists regularly attacked British influence, though Christina often disapproved of articles and cartoons belittling the Chinese, Indians, Jews and Aborigines. She was particularly displeased when in 1886 the then editor, James Edmond, changed *The Bulletin*'s nationalist banner from "Australia for Australian" to "Australia for the White Men". Christina also found his articles of justification unsettling. She was a strong believer, and in some circumstances, spokesperson for not only the equality for the sexes, but also classes and racial groups. One of Edmond's articles stated, "By Australian we mean — white men who have come to these shores — with clean records." She saw this in direct conflict with her stance on equality and another example of openly diminishing against the role played by ex-convicts and descendants of convicts.

Though Joseph was annoyed at Traill's departure, Christina was pleased with some of the changes he made at *The Bulletin*. She enjoyed the emerging literary nationalism known as The Bulletin School, with its bush poets. She especially liked The Bulletin Debate, a well-publicised dispute between two poets, Henry Lawson and Banjo Patterson. The debate took place via a series of poems about the merits of living in the Australian bush. Except for a trip to Lithgow and others into the Hawkesbury Valley, Christina had not ventured far beyond the settled area around the harbour. She was fascinated that two men could present such different images, Patterson tending to romanticise bush life while Lawson represented country life as doom and gloom. Though she enjoyed their work Christina was delighted that a woman was also a respected contributor to The Bulletin School. Mary Gilmore was a fiery radical poet, a champion of the workers and the oppressed. Christina admired her stance on society and Gilmore's call for utopian socialism, where there was no need for class struggle or social revolution. Based on her experiences with the social classes in the colony Christina wasn't sure that people from the supposed upper classes could voluntarily adopt a cooperative approach to change. The divide between the free and convict heritage seemed too wide. The attitude of the British to almost every other nation was openly ethnocentric and attitude to women, chauvinistic.

# Chapter 37

Joseph felt honoured to be elected a delegate to the first intercolonial conference of Chambers of Manufactures, 5th to 7th October 1887 in Adelaide. The following year he would also attended a subsequent conference in Melbourne. His involvement had resulted from being at a meeting in the Sydney Town Hall when the NSW chamber had been formed and Archibald Forsyth elected as president. The chief motivation on each occasion was to work for intercolonial free trade and uniform tariffs.

Joseph was pleased to be with like-minded men and moved a motion that "Australian patents for new products and processes should allow only for the article to be manufactured in Australia." He was strongly supported as was the motion that any patents developed in the colonies should apply to the whole of Australia not just the colony in which it is lodged.

Christina was displeased that Joseph had not asked her if she wished to accompany him to the Adelaide conference. Several of her acquaintances planned to make the trip as the conference offered a program for "the ladies", even though it was purely social. Following the death of their infant son Elijah Ross in April and the fact that Joseph had announced that their son Thomas, who was now twenty-one, was to caretake the business in his absence, Christina announced she would be travelling with Joseph. His reaction was more of dismay that disapproval, he had just assumed she would not be interested.

This created a dilemma when Christina's friends made it very clear that her wardrobe was not suitable for such an occasion. Though of good quality, they were sadly out of date. With little time to prepare, the decision was made to purchase directly from a local department store rather than have outfits made. Under Louise Dutruc's guidance, Christina and three friends spent an enjoyable afternoon at the David Jones department store in George Street. The first problem was that all Christina's day and evening dresses featured protruding bustles that were out of fashion. Thus two evening gowns and three day dresses were purchased with the new bell-shaped skirts, gored to fit smoothly over the hips, and bodices marked with large leg-o-mutton or gigot sleeves. As hats were an all-important accessory, three were purchased, all wide and heavily trimmed with a range of feathers, flowers and ribbons. With her new style, Christina also had to obtain a new jacket that featured the gigot style. As her friends were concerned about cool evenings, two capes were added that gracefully fell over Christina's shoulders and were trimmed with jet beading, braid and fur.

Christina insisted her shoes would be adequate but was eager to purchase a range of gloves for both day and evening wear. She was certain that none of the other ladies would have callused hands, hers from shovelling coal into the furnaces and sweeping the factory floor. She was also conscious of the black coal strains around her nails. No matter how much she scrubbed them, or soaked them in lemon juice they never came completely clean.

Joseph was happy to pack in a large carpet bag but Christina insisted on the purchase of a new trunk and matching large hatbox. Though Joseph considered this an extravagance, Christina rarely spent money on herself and how she looked in public was important to his ego as it reflected on his standing among a group of men who supported his position in the chamber.

The trip could now be done completely by train as the Melbourne to Adelaide railway line, the Intercolonial Express, had opened that year. Prior to this it would have meant taking a coastal cruise from Melbourne to Adelaide or a long overland trip in uncomfortable stage coaches. The new railway development had been made simpler as both the Victorian and South Australian colonies had adopted the Irish broad-gauge rails at five feet three inches.

The first leg was by steam train from Sydney to Albury, located on the Murray River and the border between the colonies of NSW and Victoria. The Sydney terminus that had started as a tin shed on the site of Cleveland Paddock, Redfern had been built in 1855 but a new station had been constructed on the same site in 1874. Christina was impressed by the brick and stone station though the dirt road leading up to it was rough and clogged with wagons carrying every imaginable type of merchandise. Their first-class carriage was very comfortable, and Christina enjoyed an acceptable meal in the dining car. She was impressed that the train had a lady's lavatory with drop holes onto the tracks and two wash bowls. Toilet paper had to be purchased from the conductor in plain brown wrappers as the product was considered too delicate for public discussion. She was certain that the same level of facilities and service was not offered in the second-class carriages.

In 1883, the New South Wales and Victorian colonial governments had finally agreed to build a bridge over the Murray River with the Victorian wide gauge railway used to cross and meet at Albury. Here passengers changed for a train bound for Melbourne. NSW trains ran on the English standard gauge rails of four feet, eight and a half inches.

Christina asked a conductor on the train why the gauges were the width they are. He smiled and said it was a very long story but in short it dated back to the

Romans. They built roads with ruts for the wheels of the imperial war chariots, this distance was designed to accommodate the width of two equine buttocks, and Joseph interrupted, 'You mean two horses bottoms?'

The conductor gave a curt smile and continued. Back in England early roads also had ruts so wagon wheels were made the same distance apart. These were also adopted by the first horse-drawn trams and trains. Naturally when steam trains commenced, planners used what they knew and adopted the same distance. Christina added, 'But Victoria is different?'

Joseph again interrupted, finding the whole conversation amusing, 'So, Victoria's rail is based on the size of two pony's bums?'

'No, that was a political decision. At the time railways started in Victoria, the colony's railway engineer was F. W. Shields and he was Irish with a particular dislike for the English. In NSW, their engineer was James Wallace, a Scotsman.'

Arriving at the Melbourne terminus Christina was surprised that their station consisted of a mere collection of weatherboard sheds. However, it was well positioned in the centre of the city at Flinders Street.

The Adelaide station in North Terrace was a much grander affair. Originally built in 1856, a second storey had been added in 1878. Of the three stations this was by far the grandest. The stone building with red brick dressings had a large, arched portico and wide verandas.

Joseph had booked them into the Cohen's Family Hotel, centrally located at the corner of Rundle and Bent Streets. The promotion for the hotel had stated it had been designed by William McMinn who was the architect of the governor's summer residence, Marble House. Their room on the first floor had a wide veranda with detailed ironwork. The hotel was part of a new concept called a complex as besides the hotel the building was attached to fourteen shops that spread to the west down Rundle Street.

The wives of the various colonies delegates to the conference had been invited as the city was holding the Adelaide Jubilee International Exhibition. It was being held to celebrate the fiftieth anniversary of Queen Victoria's accession to the British throne in June 1837. It was also a celebration of the fiftieth anniversary of the Proclamation of South Australia. The delegates to the conference had been invited to arrive a few days before it commenced so the wives could attend the Grand International Band Competition that was being held that week at the exhibition.

The South Australian delegate's wives were to host their interstate visitors and it was planned to spend two days viewing the two thousand two hundred exhibits from twenty-six countries in a specially constructed exhibition building. On these days, the ladies would meet at Adelaide railway station and board a train on the line constructed for the exhibition that ran via an underpass of King Street and between the Parade Grounds and Government House. Christina was delighted by her recent purchases with positive comments both on the modern style of her dresses and the flamboyance of her new hats.

Though Christina found the displays very interesting and rather educational, she, like many of the rather prudish group, found the work of the award winner for painting rather risqué. The works of John Reinhard Weguelin, an English painter, included some landscapes with lush backgrounds but also what were called neo-classical works inspired by classical antiquity and mythology, the beautiful nymphs and mermaids clad in virtually see-through gowns or less.

Another day was a ladies lunch held in the new Adelaide Arcade. Their chaperones explained that the arcade had been designed by Latham Withall and Alfred Wells, who had also designed the Exhibition building they had visited. It too had domes with a focus on the use of glass, in the case of the arcade fifty thousand panes, which, they also boasted, had been naturally, especially made in, and shipped from London. Christina smiled as she imagined what Joseph's reaction to that comment might be. Before lunch, they explored the fifty shops and were invited to partake of a Turkish bath, located in the southeast corner of the arcade, as an afternoon experience. Christina was not surprised that they had no partakers. The speaker at their lunch was a representative from the Royal Geographical Society of Australia that had formed in 1886. He spoke about a place called Kangaroo Island but rather than talking about kangaroos his talk was on the Ligurian bees that lived on the island and produced one of the purist strains of honey in the world.

The following day their outing was to the Adelaide Zoological Gardens that had opened in 1883 and displayed birds and mammals that had previously been kept at the Botanic Gardens. The Adelaide ladies had organised an afternoon speaker, Edith Dornwell, who had been the first woman to be admitted to a university, Adelaide University in 1881, and who in 1885 had become the first woman to graduate in the science field.

Third formal outing, third new dress, Louise Dutruc's advice had been spot on. Christina had fitted right in. All were impressed by her breadth of knowledge about political and current events. Though some of the quieter "door mouse" wives considered her a little forward, all found her conversation interesting and her questions insightful.

While in Adelaide, Christina took the opportunity to attend a meeting of the South Australian branch of the Women's Christian Temperance Union that had formed the previous year. She was excitedly welcomed and made to feel very important.

As she had enjoyed the visit to Adelaide and the interaction with women of similar interests to herself, she decided that she would accompany Joseph to the 1888 convention to be held in Melbourne. However, nature had other ideas and Christina found she was again with child, Edith Mary Ross, Christina's thirteenth and last child, being born in Newtown in 1888. Unfortunately, seventeen months later Edith became a victim of one of the deadliest pandemics in history. Referred to as the Asiatic or Russian Flu, it would kill over one million people worldwide, with over six thousand deaths in Sydney. Sadly, this was still a time that the medical community clung to miasmatic theories of disease causation and the doctor they called focussed on isolation, cleaning and staying at home. The miasma theory believed that diseases were caused by a noxious form of bad air, also known as night air, often from the fumes of rotting organic matter. The doctor had talked about the disease being caused by environmental factors such as contaminated water, foul air, and poor hygienic conditions. This Christina found offensive, as she had taken every possible step the doctor had recommended when Edith became ill.

This sparked an interest in Christina, who discussed her concerns with friends in the temperance movement. One member, Violet, a nurse, talked about some reports she had read on the work in Britain by a Joseph Lister who had developed a theory about germs being responsible for diseases. Another researcher who worked in France was Louis Pasteur, who had also shown the relationship between germs and disease and suggested boric acid to kill these microorganisms before and after confinement. This only increased Christina's frustration that if a simple nurse knew this information, why didn't their doctor consider this type of research? It was true at the time hospitals were seen as a place for the poor, conditions considered chaotic, overcrowded and squalid. Free settlers saw them as places of last resort, suitable for convicts and desperate people without money. Everyone else expected to be treated by medical practitioners in their own home, where they could be nursed by family or servants. Following the death of Elijah and then Edith, Christina now questioned this practice.

Encouraged by Violet, Christina set about raising money for and supporting the Sydney Infirmary and Dispensary. Violet had done her training there and talked about the amazing work of Lucy Osburn, lady superintendent of the Sydney Infirmary, who had come to Sydney in the late 1860s at the request of the then Colonial Secretary, Henry Parkes. He had written to the British nursing pioneer, Florence Nightingale, requesting she send out trained nurses due to the scandalous state of the Sydney Infirmary.

Lucy and five other nurses were sent by the Nightingale Fund Council, arriving in Sydney on 5th March 1868 and were employed by the NSW Government on three-year contracts.

In 1873, a Royal Commission into Public Charities had condemned the conditions at the Sydney Infirmary and vindicated Osburn's efforts to make improvement. Osburn had also gained considerable status in the colony in that a week after she arrived, she had to attend to a royal patient. When Prince Alfred, Duke of Edinburgh, son of Queen Victoria was visiting Sydney in March 1868 he had been wounded by a would-be-assassin at Clontarf. Though she nursed him at Government House rather than the Sydney Infirmary it gave her and her staff the credibility they needed. Naturally Christina had heard of the event, it had featured in the local papers. In January 1868, she and Joseph had joined what seemed thousands of others to watch the fireworks display on the harbour shore to welcome the prince. He was on a world tour on the steam frigate HMS *Galatea*. At the time, the Ross's were aware of simmering sectarian tension in the colonies. Even in their own glassworks there had been minor altercations between some Irish Catholic and non-Catholic men. Prior to the shooting at Clontarf, people had been aware, through newspaper reports, of Fenian terrorism in England.

In 1881, royal assent had been given to the Sydney Hospital Act for the building of a new hospital and it was this Christina put her efforts towards. She had hoped to meet Lucy, but was told Lucy had returned to England in 1884 but was still nursing among the sick and poor in London. Christina did get to meet Miss McKay, who had replaced Lucy at the hospital, and described Lucy as an exceptional woman, who considered nursing as the highest employment, but requiring a spirit of devotion. Miss McKay could remember her saying, 'You nurses should exist for patients, not they for you.' Miss McKay felt that her work and dedication had laid the foundation of modern nursing in Australia and pioneered the employment of high-status professional women in public institutions.

Though Christina and her son Thomas had been at odds for years, due to her disapproval of his lifestyle and business dealings, Thomas admired his mother's empathy to what she saw as the less fortunate. In later years, he would credit his mother for his leading role in the development of the South Sydney Hospital.

# Chapter 38

The Chamber of Manufacturing itself got off to a slow start, mostly because its supporters focussed most of their attention on lobbying for tariff protection, which many manufacturers did not feel the need to support. Others were concerned about the call to set up a Protection Union, in direct opposition to the Free Traders, led by Sir Henry Parkes. Parkes had become the premier of NSW in 1872 and was a supporter of free trade. During his first administration, he reduced the import duties in NSW that virtually made it a free trade colony. Being a shopkeeper in Hunter Street, free trade suited him as all his merchandise was imported thus duty free increased his profit margin. Parkes and Joseph also differed on the concept of border duties. Again, as a merchant free trade between the colonies was considered beneficial but for Joseph his major competition were bottles manufactured in Victoria. Of equal quality and actually cheaper per unit it was the high intercolonial duties that helped Joseph as it made the Victorian product uneconomic for NSW manufacturers to use. Though industrial protection was the chamber's focus, it introduced a new constitution to maintain a non-political stance hoping it could also champion the broad interest of NSW businesses. It wished to be independent and wanted to maintain a not-for-profit identity. Though debates and motions often tended to be unrealistic, at heart the Chamber wanted practical policy solutions to ensure businesses across NSW could prosper and grow. The idea was not new, the Sydney Chamber of Commerce had existed since 1826. It had been established as a local network society to represent businesses across Greater Sydney and to advocate for public policies to enhance Sydney as a competitive, and liveable city. Joseph had seen some benefits in its capacity to encourage networks but as he was trying to expand his market both with Sydney but also to country towns and the other colonies, he found the idea of a local Chamber of Commerce limiting.

# Chapter 39

In 1888, their business, now known as Australian Perseverance Glass Bottle Works, employed family and up to forty men and boys. It advertised the most modern appliances and machinery for the perfect manufacture of bottle glass.

A newspaper article written by Christina stated:

"The works, which have been appropriately named the Perseverance Glass Bottle Works, cover a large area of ground, and though the number of hands employed is large, many more could be taken on were the demand for the products greater. There are three smelting furnaces, having tanks capable of holding thirty, sixteen, and four tons of liquid glass respectively and nine annealing ovens. The amount of coal consumed is slightly more than two hundred tons per month, and some idea of the intensity of the heat that is maintained in the main furnaces can be formed considering the temperature reached amounts of many thousands of degrees Fahrenheit. It may be mentioned that the stones at the bottom of the large glass tanks are of the best Pyrmont sandstone, while the sides and crown are of English fire bricks. Based on Joseph's extensive experience in England, Europe, and America, he considered none of these areas in the glassmaking world had the same quality of the principal ingredients, the quality of local lime and sand being so high. Joseph contends that Marulan lime was the finest in the world."

Despite a growing industrial sector and demand, Joseph was again declared bankrupt, with creditors including his son Robert and he also owed one hundred pounds to Edward Voltaire Price, who did all Joseph's posters and handbills, and was also the future father-in-law of his son Francis Ross. Joseph cited the inability to compete against cheap imported articles as the reason for the failure. He was unable to pay most of his creditors and also many of his employees. He owed coal merchants, soda ash suppliers, suppliers of the rubber washers used in capping, Pyrmont quarry for unpaid sandstone deliveries. As Joseph insisted his customers pay for their bottles prior to manufacture, thus able to use the money to cover costs of raw materials, they too formed part of his creditors.

# Chapter 40

To get his business up and running again, Christina encouraged Joseph to again take advantage of the newspapers. Unlike some specialist manufacturers, he had worked in Europe and America and saw the benefits of his factory churning out whatever size or type of bottle customers wanted. He also promoted the range of colours with clear, blue, green, olive, black, amber and white. In 1889, Christina had written a series of advertisement for Joseph, as J Ross and Sons, advertising "patent bottles of every description fitted with English stoppers with glass, marble and rubber rings." Their promotion also advertising themselves as the "oldest glassworks in Australia."

Joseph was determined not to fail again, so instigated the formation of a company to be called The Ross Manufacturing Company. However, the world and especially Australia, was heading for a depression thus usual sources of overseas funding dried up and banks greatly reduced their lending.

With Joseph engrossed in production and sales, Christina found it necessary to monitor both the finances and labour supply. She had noted an increase in the interest of some men to become part of the growing union movement. A representative of The Australian Glass Bottle Maker's Union had visited their factory several times in the 1880s. There was little interest among the men as though not necessarily happy with wages and conditions, they at least had a job. As the union was not registered with the colonial government, Christina saw little threat, but made sure her sons were aware of the impact unionisation might have. The movement gained a greater focus when the NSW branch of the Australian Glass Workers Union was established in Sydney in 1894 as the Amalgamated Glass Bottle Makers' Trade Protection Society of Australia.

The economic depression of the 1890s had increased business conservatism and a desire to curtail the power of the growing union movement. Christina's son Thomas focussed on management and was on the side of the employer group, actively discouraging the men from engaging with the union. He blocked any meetings and made it clear that the Ross's would not employ any men who were part of the union organisation. Son Frank, on the other hand, focussed his attention on hands-on production and felt a close bond with the men. He spent his days working alongside them, heard their gripes and complaints. Frank understood how tough life was on a fixed wage that, for most, was only paid monthly. Often excuses were given by Thomas when payments were delayed. Frank had been welcomed into the men's dwellings and had seen the abysmal living conditions that many of them had to go home to each evening. He reflected on his own life, living in a house owned by his mother, eating the nourishing lunch that was delivered each day to the factory by his mother's housekeeper, never feeling hungry. The social disparity was great. Though he would call himself a member of the working-class, Frank was conscious that the term contained a great divide. On Sunday he would don his weekend status, heading off to the Wesleyan church service and outings, mixing with those of money and position. He had an interest in a particular girl, Edith, the daughter of a prominent family, her father a successful miner and publican living in Arncliffe. Frank knew it was his family's business interests that made him acceptable, his future father-in-law had even lent Joseph money to expand his business. Edith, an independent woman like his mother had trained as a spectacle maker and repairer with Henry Frost in George Street Sydney. Though the families made the usual plans, their wedding took place in her father's home, as five months later Frank's son James Clyde Ross was born.

Though looking very similar, being tall, blue eyed with brown slightly curled hair, both with thick moustaches, the brothers were very different. While Thomas worked in collared shirt and jacket, Frank preferred his open necked flannel shirt and vest. Thomas was ambitious, often investigating future options while Frank was happy with his lot. He was a good glass blower and enjoyed the company of the men. He worked hard but felt that was a man's role and duty in life. To an outsider the two reflected the fierce class war that was raging, the ruthlessness and even greed of Thomas in unrestrained business interests compared to Frank's calm relaxed approach, seeming happy to be valued and respected in the family business.

# Chapter 41

In 1889, the business changed its name to Joseph Ross and Son, a name used till 1893 when Joseph took on a new partner Edward Samuels and traded under J Ross and Co. Business was good and by the end of the year Joseph bought out Samuels and again was a sole trader.

Christina was devastated when a few months later Joseph suffered a stroke that left him slightly incapacitated. Though it had not affected his mental capacity, it resulted in speech difficulties and he was no longer able to do the very physical work required. This resulted in him retreating to his office spending hours reading newspapers and journals, often sleeping in a cot in a back room. As with most of their married life Christina had to step up, now not only caring for her family and ensuring that there was sufficient money set aside in her name to support when necessary, but also rising with her sons early each morning to stoke the furnaces. Though Christina took oversight of all aspects of the operation, Thomas and Frank were given greater control of the day to day running of the factory. Thomas who had a longer period of formal education had never been interested in learning the practical side of the business focussed on the management and administration side. Frank who had learnt every process, became production and floor manager.

The family had always been expected to work in the business, the boys learning the trade while the girls acted as cleaners.

Christina believed in keeping up with the times so oversaw the introduction of the crown cap, a metal disk with crimped edges which could be pushed around the bead rim of the bottle. This was soon followed by the introduction of another innovation, the screw-top closure with a thread moulded on the inside of the neck and a corresponding threaded cork.

# Chapter 42

Despite some initial protest by her sons, Christina led the negotiations for the company to be sold to the Australian Drug Company. This had resulted partly from Joseph's health and his need to retire but was also a calculated business move by Christina who could see that the area in which the factory was located was becoming a densely populated residential suburb and it was clear that the Newtown Municipal Council was moving to close industries. Large tracts of land were being cleared for housing development. After the sale, the factory was torn down, a plan by the Australian Drug Company to reduce competition with its North Botany (Mascot) bottle works.

As part of the sale to the Australian Drug Company, Joseph had agree not to open another glass business for ten years, however within three months, with their mothers financial support and encouragement, sons Thomas and Frank opened Ross Brother's bottle factory and kiln in Bray Street, Erskineville.

The land had previously been a dairy farm, but had identified by Frank Ross, who was living at 10

Bray Street, as a potential location for a new glass factory. Christina saw this as a positive omen, an area of Sydney named after Erskine Villa, the house of the Wesleyan minister, Reverend George Erskine, built in 1830. The area was originally incorporated in 1872 with the name Municipal District of Macdonald Town. In 1893 it was renamed Erskineville, when the Parliament of NSW passed the Borough of Erskineville Act. As the area already had Bakewell Brothers, a two-storey brick factory and boots and tanning factories as established industries, a glass works would fit in. The site was surrounded by rows of small three-metre-wide Victorian terraces, like the one Frank lived in, that were the homes of the workers in these industries and Christina realised the locals would welcome additional employment opportunities.

Christina contributed three-fifths of the capital, the sons one-fifth each. Some of the money had come from the sale of the Camperdown site but most was from Christina who by this time was independently financially secure. Though the younger brother Alexander, now aged fourteen, worked at the new factory, he was too young to join the partnership and John was only ten and attending Erskineville Primary School that had opened in 1881.

The block on which the factory was built consisted of about six to eight housing blocks, a frontage of 36.5 metres and depth 30.4 metres fronting Bray Street and backing onto Devine Street. Taking up about seventy-five percent of the block the factory had a large, corrugated iron roof with a central obelisk-like brick chimney. Under the roof a furnace, six ovens, storerooms, dry storage area for coal, chemical cellars, engineer's workshop, packing areas, loading bays, an office and stable. The office of the new factory, officially at 43 Bray Street, was a raised section with windows looking out to the street but also a large glass wall overlooking the factory floor. It is here Joseph would spend his days. He would arrive at six thirty a.m., wandering in to check that the processes were being carried out correctly then sitting in his swivel chair performing some simple clerical duties.

On a shelf in the office Joseph kept an array of bottles filled with boiled lollies. Some days after school local children, mostly those of employees, would gather in the loading dock and Joseph would distribute some of the treats. Though to his own children Joseph had been a strict and demanding task master and a ruthless employer, to his young apprentices he had a senses of community responsibility. For many years prior to his stroke, he had run the local Band of Hope meetings. This was a structure founded by the Leeds temperance society, of England. Its role was to teach children the importance of sobriety at a time when many of them were living in poverty due to their parent's alcoholism. He also used the time to preach on his own work ethic. With his favourite whisky in the office cupboard and as a major producer of wine and beer bottles, some would see this as being rather hypocritical. Joseph rationalised it as his attempt to balance the books, make a living yet keeping a link to his Wesleyan origins. Joseph could still sing Hymn 403 from the 1846 *Wesleyan Methodist Connection.*

"Touch not with the poison thy lips,
If thou wouldst be free from its pain;
For he is in danger who sips,
He only safe who abstains."

On another shelf Joseph would keep what he called his medications. Bicarbonate of soda was used for his regular stomach upsets and for anything else a bottle of laudanum relieved the pain. This opium-based liquid was freely available from any pharmacy. Unfortunately, Joseph suffered discomfort and constant pain as the early symptoms of prostate cancer took hold.

While Christina, Thomas, Frank and the factory's employees worked around him Joseph would enjoy a full breakfast and hot midday meal delivered to him by the live-in housekeeper. She would return at three p.m. with hot brewed tea and buttered bread with Joseph insisting that all family members be on site to partake. Though his speech were slurred by the partial paralysis of his face, he still barked orders and expected family to follow his sometime irrational and contradictory instructions.

Christina made sure that each day she would share lunch with her daughter Josephine and youngest sons John and Alexander. The family's two-storey home at 70 Bray Street, part of three double-storey terraces known as Albert Terraces was only one hundred metres down the street, and this was her attempt to spend some quality time with her children.

On the 27th of February 1895 Frank Ross was married to Edith Mary Price by the Presbyterian minister Rev. Gardiner at Arncliffe. They were married in the residence of Edward Voltaire Price, the witnesses being Andrew Boag and Christina Ross. Their son James Clyde Ross born in the family home at 23 Bray Street, was the only one of Frank's eleven children who would enter the glass business.

# Chapter 43

Almost from the beginning of Ross Brothers, conflict was apparent between the two brothers. Christina attempted but had little success in settling the constant disagreements between Thomas and Frank.

Thomas's excuse was usually based on the interference by his father Joseph and his constant attempt to micromanage a business that he was technically no longer a part of.

Frank however blamed the problems on Thomas's drunkenness. He complained that Thomas would just not come to work and at one stage he and his mother had not seen him for over three months. Around the same time Thomas's wife had left him due to his drunken habits. Ann took Thomas to court suing her estranged husband for assault, desertion and maintenance. She had reports from family, neighbours and a doctor showing that Thomas had a vile temper and often beat her. In the court case a Stanmore doctor stated that on one occasion he had been called to their home as Ann had miscarried. He expressed concern that this could be related to the alleged physical violence by Thomas.

Frank also expressed concern over the way his brother was handling the company books. Frank had discovered money from the business going into the account of Thomas Ross rather than Ross Brothers. Thomas tried to justify this by saying it was easier to pay some creditors from his own personal accounts and would have reimbursed the Ross Brothers account at a later stage. Thomas often took the business financial books home and refused to allow his partners, Christina and Frank, access to them. Despite a court decree, Thomas remained defiant and his refusal to have the books audited did nothing to allay their suspicions.

# Chapter 44

During this time Christina maintained her support for the women's movement. She attended a meeting in Sydney Town Hall where the National Council of Women of New South Wales was founded. Its formation was largely instigated by Margaret Windeyer, its first honorary secretary, supported by Rose Scott, who was a member of the executive committee and also served as international secretary. The eleven original affiliated groups outlined a very broad agenda. These were to promote the social, civil, moral and religious welfare of the community; to work for the removal of all inequalities of women, whether legal, economic or social and to promote such conditions of life as would assure every child an opportunity for full and free development. Christina didn't mind that the council was dominated by women of the middle and upper classes. Its first five presidents being wives or daughters of the incumbent governors of NSW. She realised that these women had the time and connections to provide the best opportunity for success.

The union was a non-party, non-sectarian, umbrella organisation for a large and diverse number of affiliated women's organisations. It functioned as a political lobby group, particularly for the interests of women and children, attempting to influence local, state and federal government, and as a coordinating body to enable concerted effort on specific issues. The council emerged as a largely middle-class women's organisation, a major focal point for women's activism.

The council operated through a standing committee system whereby specific issues were brought before the council, and if there was general agreement that an issue should be taken up, a subcommittee was established to investigate the matter. Women's suffrage was the first issue taken up by the council, but other early concerns included the provision of Domestic Economy classes in public schools; temperance; the need for Women Factory Inspectors; improved working conditions for women; and the establishment of kindergartens and nursery schools. Christina was particularly active in two subcommittees, the first related to her work in the temperance movement, the second the subcommittee for the improved working conditions for women. As she and her family were the only females at the glass factory and very few of their clients employed women, she felt no conflict in demanding action in other local factories. She helped organise pickets at local clothing manufacturers and boot making factories and with her daughter Christine handed out pamphlets demanding better pay and safer conditions.

While supporting the union, Christina had developed a close friendship with Susannah Maybanke Salfe. Susannah had arrived with her family from Surrey in 1854. They moved into a rented cottage in the Rocks. Susannah was training as a teacher when the Ross's arrived to live with Joseph's brother, Thomas. Both women enjoyed afternoon strolls along the waterfront, talking about the people they passed, their lives and difference from their homeland. In 1867 at St Phillip's Anglican Church on Church Hill, Susannah had married Edmund Wolstenholme, a timber merchant who lived in Maitland. Though their first child Harry was born in Maitland, the family moved to Balmain, again close to where Christina was living at the Brown glass factory. Edmund had set himself up as an accountant and Christina organised for him to do some accountancy work for Joseph's glass factory. Unfortunately, Wolstenholme was to become an unemployed alcoholic and deserted his wife in 1884.

Susannah, like Christina was determined to dictate her own destiny. Because of the law at the time, Susannah was unable to divorce Wolstenholme. This injustice within the legal system gave men all rights, women none. Divorce was only on the grounds of adultery, which was hard to prove. She had no rights to her children or to her own earnings within the marriage, she could not leave her property to her children. Christina supported her in her campaign for women's rights to divorce that led to the passage of the Divorce Amendment and Extension Act in 1892. Initially, Susannah had taken in boarders, which reduced some of their financial problems, then established her own girls' school, Maybanke College in Frazer Street, Marrickville. She built up a solid reputation based upon the success of her pupils. From 1891, Susannah was a foundation vice-president of the Womanhood Suffrage League of New South Wales, becoming president in 1893. She was also a member of the Women's Literary Society. From 1894 she began publishing and editing her own fortnightly paper, *Woman's Voice*. Though the magazine only remained in print for eighteen months, Christina took time to read each publication. She found that it took a clear and logical approach, not as affronting and revolutionary as some other women's movement publications.

In March 1899, Susannah married (Sir) Francis Anderson, professor of philosophy at the University of Sydney. She became active in the National Council of Women of New South Wales, and heavily involved with the activities of the University Women's Society.

# Chapter 45

On the 13th of October 1896, Christina Ross instigated a suit in the Equity Court against her sons. Though she knew that it was Thomas that was the problem, she had other children to consider and wanted to retrieve the one hundred pounds sterling she had lent both Thomas and Frank that had been shown as their contribution to the business. Once the business was established, she had advanced a further seven hundred pounds sterling when cash flow problems had occurred and though she had demanded the repayment of these amounts that had not occurred. She asked the court to have a receiver appointed to sell the business and the goodwill that came with the Ross glass name. The one thousand two hundred pounds sterling Christina had invested of her own money was a very large sum at that time (approximately three hundred and ten thousand Australian dollars in 2020s terms).

Thomas, as business manager, denied that he had kept incorrect books or refused his mother access to them. Frank was put in the awkward position of knowing there was a problem but trying to protect the business that was his livelihood. Thomas claimed that it was because his mother refused to sign cheques related to the business, that he had been forced to open another account to which she was not signatory. Frank, as factory manager, stated that his mother had insisted on taking charge of the furnaces and as a result around twenty-five pounds sterling worth of bottles were spoiled each week, but as she was the major partner, he had not felt that he had the power to stop her.

A large part of the problem was that the business had been set up as a simple family partnership and not a formal joint stock company. It was basically based on a handshake with the agreement to use family funds.

As a result of the court case in October 1896, a decree was given that the partnership was officially dissolved and that Thomas and Frank both had to pay back four hundred pounds sterling in weekly instalments of four pounds. Christina was given the ownership of the factory and all its equipment with the power to appoint a receiver and manager for the business and she did, her husband Joseph Ross Senior. With his poor state of health, she now had full control of the business and all its assets.

From the very beginning when Joseph had worked with Professor Morris Birkbeck Pell, Christina had read and kept copies of all information and reports on the production of glass and bottle making. Being a traditionalist, Joseph would only give a cursory glance at articles about new technology and mechanisation. However Christina filed each one and decided that they made an excellent resource that she shared with her sons. Frank was like his father, so old ways were the best. Thomas only saw financial outlay so didn't consider such expenditure as relevant. It was Alexander and John who shared their mother's interest and she actually used some of the articles when helping the younger boys during their learning to read.

Christina also tried to keep abreast of modernisation. She managed to obtain copies of European and American journals such as *The Journal of the Society of Chemical Industry*, which looked at patents and developments in plants, apparatus and machinery. These she studied, again encouraging her sons to consider the ideas in terms of their own glass business.

The conflict between Thomas and Frank deteriorated to such a degree that by mid July 1897 Frank left the business, taking a position at another glassworks. It now technically became the responsibility of Alexander and John to take over the running of the business. At the time, the factory employed twenty-two men and boys, most full time but some specialists like glass blowers were engaged as pieceworkers. At that time, Alexander and John were also shown as employees, John earning two pounds and ten shillings a week and Alexander paid as an apprentice earning fifteen shillings a week. Christina now focussed her attention on John as his ideas about the future had been moulded by, and reflected, her own beliefs.

Thomas, after leaving, worked on re-establishing his business reputation and also attempted to make amends to his wife and family. In 1884, Thomas had been shown as sales manager for Joseph Ross and Sons Glass. However, after 1894, instead of joining John and Alexander in Ross Bros, Thomas had moved from the family.

Thomas Ross was not discharged from bankruptcy until January 1901 and though not legally allowed to hold business interests, in January 1900 he acquired a major shareholding in Alexandria Glass Bottle Works Ltd. In July 1903 in partnership with a Scottish-born master glass blower, David Vance, Thomas opened The Australian Glass Bottle Works, specialising in medical bottles, fruit preserving jars and whisky bottles.

Vance had arrived in Sydney about 1886 with his wife Catherine, née Hutton, whom he had married on the 24th of April 1885 at Glasgow. Vance had worked for the Australian Drug Co. at its North Botany bottle works and then acquired two small glass-foundries at Waterloo.

A Freemason and a justice of the peace, Thomas had learned his politics in the tight little world of

Camperdown and Newtown and followed his father as a committee member of the Chamber of Manufactures. In 1908-09 he was mayor of Waterloo. He was recruited by (Sir) James Joynton Smith as senior vice-president and government nominee on the board of South Sydney Hospital in 1909. His wife Ann-Elizabeth joined the board in January 1913. In 1910 Thomas failed to win Liberal pre-selection for the State seat of Botany.

Thomas vigorously advocated a subsidy for the local brass band, stressing the great pleasure residents derived from musical selections played in Waterloo Park. He was a promoter of the Alexandria-Waterloo Working Men's Institute opened on 31 August 1908, with its library and other recreational facilities.

Australian Glass Manufacturers Co. Ltd (AGM) bought out Vance and Ross in 1915, paying the partners twenty-four thousand pounds in cash. As well, Vance received nine thousand AGM shares and Ross seven thousand. The Alexandria plant was demolished. Ross, in poor health for some years, retired to Burraneer Bay, Cronulla, naming his home Bottles.

When AGM was registered in 1913 it was the amalgamation of the Waterloo Glass Bottle Works Ltd and the Melbourne Glass Bottle Works Co Pty Ltd. AGM had purchased the business of Vance and Ross Pty Ltd and absorbed the Zetland Glass Bottle Works Ltd to reduce competition. In 1921, AGM had largely obtained a monopoly of the bottle making trade of Australia. It had taken this step as the minister for Customs had announced a plan to place higher tariffs on imported sheet glass. To combat this, AGM like many similar industries faced with higher tariffs, increased domestic production.

In the 1920s, Vance moved to Glen Nevis, next door, where he died on 25 August 1931. An ardent promoter of Empire Day, Ross had celebrated the end of World War One by creating a large mosaic of three flags from coloured bottle glass set in concrete at his front gate, in honour of and relief at the survival of his sons Flight Lieutenant Frederick and Lance Corporal Thomas (who had won the Military Medal) and of a nephew. Thomas Ross died on 28 December 1936 at his residence, Bottles, Woolooware Road, Cronulla, aged seventy-one years and he was buried at Woronora Cemetery.

Both Thomas's sons worked for the AGM's subsidiary Crown Crystal Glass Pty Ltd, set up in 1926 to make cut glass, lighting ware and Pyrex. Young Tom became commercial manager. A stocky, hard-faced man, he presided over the works' cricket team, its golf days and its annual ball and represented the company in court against the trade unions. In 1955, however, the board tried to force his resignation, perhaps because of his ill health, and when he refused, dismissed him. He died at his Bellevue Hill home on 18 February 1963.

Legends he and his father had elaborated about their family as pioneer glassmakers, into which they had adopted Vance, were accepted by AGM (later Australian Consolidated Industries Ltd) without question as part of its corporate history.

An announcement in *The Propeller*, Hurstville, N.S.W. 31st December 1936:

"Death of Mr Thomas Ross

Mr Thomas Ross, who died last Sunday at his home, Bottles, Burraneer Bay, Cronulla, aged 71 years, was the son of Mr Joseph Ross, the pioneer bottle and glass manufacturer of Australia. Mr Thomas Ross also went into the glass manufacturing business, and became a principal in the business of Messrs Vance and Ross which, in 1916, amalgamated with the Sydney Glass and Bottle Works, the Waterloo Glass and Bottle Works, the Melbourne Glass and Bottle Works, and the Adelaide Glass and Bottle Works, to form the Australian Glass Manufacturers Co., Ltd. Mr Thomas Ross retired from business many years ago because of ill-health. He was a leading figure in the establishment of the South Sydney Hospital and helped to introduce the Empire Day celebrations into the public schools of New South Wales. He is survived by Mrs Ross and two sons, Messrs Fred, and Tom Ross, both of whom are associated with the Crown Crystal Glass Co., Ltd."

The family and Sydney society had chosen to ignore previous misdemeanours. Thomas had recreated himself, the family conflict in his past, but the bonds had been broken and contact with his mother and siblings reserved to formal occasions.

# Chapter 46

Disaster again struck the family with the factory burnt to the ground in the early hours of a cold September morning in 1897.

The fire had first been noticed by the night watchman, but it was Joseph Senior who raised the alarm. As the factory was constructed of weatherboard, the fire spread quickly, the factory totally destroyed. The fire also claimed a cottage next door that was owned by an elderly man who used to own the dairy farm on which it was built. Fortunately, one account that Thomas had paid was the insurance and though it was estimated that losses amounted to eight hundred and seventy-five pounds sterling, the insurance paid four hundred and fifty pounds sterling. This was enough, and within a few weeks the factory was in production again. Christina placed an advertisement in the paper: "Ross Brothers, the invincible glassmakers, have now resumed work."

Despite their differences, after the fire Frank returned to the business to help his family rebuild. Another outcome was that Frank and his father started a new set of books that Thomas had no access to. In retaliation, in early November 1897, Thomas attempted to have Frank arrested, claiming he had misappropriated money by stealing bottles and selling them to another outlet. The claim was proved untrue, Thomas putting it down as a misunderstanding brought on by a lack of communication with him. Within days, Thomas left the business but under a cloud, as a consignment of bottles to the Australian Wine Company were not to specification and were returned, the bottles to be resold and the payment going to the wine company. No record of the moneys from this sale could be found, but the wine company later tried to claim the money owing from the estate of Thomas Ross.

With mounting debts and no employment, Thomas was forced to declare himself bankrupt. With his wife and family estranged he was forced to sell his Station Street home and move into a boarding house. Realising that she was not going to be able to regain her money from Thomas, Thomas's wife lodged a claim against Frank who, six days after Thomas, also declared himself bankrupt.

Though Christina had found the media, especially newspapers, very useful in the promotion and support of the family business, she was horrified in March 1901 when a tell-all article exposed the drunkenness, physical conflict and failure of Thomas's marriage. It referred to his temper, his beating of his wife, the fact she had left him twelve times, and the fact that she feared him and trembled every time he entered the house. Despite this, they never divorced. Christina was emotionally disturbed at the situation but was aware there were problems and that these had been reflected in his work and interaction with the other members of their family. She knew Frank had many arguments with Thomas about his drinking and though she wasn't close to Ann-Elizabeth she had organised for the housekeeper to take her and the children food and a little money to help them. For Christina, it was the fact the paper mentioned Ross Brothers. It did say he had left the company and was working as a manager of the Australian Glass Bottle Works, but she knew the very mention of Ross Brothers just added to the negativity that many other businesses felt towards them. At the time, some of their biggest customers included soft drink manufacturer J Schweppes & Co, beer brewer Tooth & Co Ltd (who by 1912 made up fifty percent of bottle demand) and Newling Brothers.

Schweppes had been a customer since it opened its first Australian factory in 1877. By then. Schweppes was nearly one hundred years old, having been started by Jacob Schweppes, a watchmaker and amateur scientist, in 1781 in Geneva, Switzerland. He had perfected the way of capturing bubbles in a bottle, a process called carbonation, but to him, "Schweppervescence." As he worked on improving his process, he gave his medicated water free to doctors in his town so they could supply their poorer patients. The company expanded into England in 1792 setting up a factory at 141 Drury Lane, a poor part of London, selling his carbonated water. Doctors there also endorsed it as a treatment for various ailments. Sometime in the mid1790s, the term "soda water" came into popular use. The water was recommended for complaints of the kidney or bladder, acidity, indigestion and gout. In 1798, Jacob sold the right to the process, but the Schweppes name remained. By the 1820s, soda water was being exported and in 1835 lemonade was added to the company's stock range. When Schweppes opened a factory in Sydney, Joseph's glass factory was supplying them bottles for soda water, lemonade, Indian Water and ginger ale.

Christina and Joseph were very pleased to have Schweppes as a customer. Their reputation reflected well on the Ross's. Joseph could remember as a young apprentice hearing about the 1851 Great Exhibition in London that was a purpose-built glass and iron structure erected in Hyde Park, known as the Crystal Palace. Schweppes was an exhibitor and also a sponsor of the exhibition, paying five thousand five hundred pounds sterling (equal current value of about one million two hundred thousand Australian dollars.) In return, Schweppes was given the sole right to be supplier of refreshments at the exhibition.

After Thomas's departure from the firm in 1897, each of the remaining brothers had a term as manager. Frank first but after his bankruptcy, John. When he had to be absent on business, Alexander assumed control, but of all the managers, he was the most disliked. He would work with the men for part of the day then walk home, change into a clean shirt collar and tie and also a different personality. He was abrupt, hissing orders, totally authoritarian. As most of the men were employed on piecework and only paid for what they made, they would ignore and even laugh at him, going on with what they were doing at their own pace. For this reason, it tended to be family, including Frank's son James, who now worked in the firm that was the target of Alexander's aggression and resentment of the other men.

This again added tension to the family dynamic with James relating these incidents to his father who would abuse and threaten Alexander.

The abuse of boys, under sixteen years, was common. Though there were regulations to protect them, these were often overlooked. This can be seen in a court case reported on in the *Sydney Morning Herald*, N.S.W. on 27th May 1903.

"A Glass Manufacturer Fined.

At the Redfern Police Court yesterday, before Mr Payten, S.M. Walter, J Taylor, of the Department of Labour and Industry, proceeded against Haigh

Zlotkowski manager of the Australian Glass Manufacturing Company, on six charges of employing a male person under the age of 16 years in that part of his works at Alexandria in the process of melting and annealing glass was carried on. Defendant pleaded not guilty. Evidence was also given by several of the boys, all of whom stated that they were, on the day the inspector called, engaged at work between the furnace and the annealing ovens. Some were drawing bottles out of the oven; others were knocking bottles off the blowpipe onto a plate. The defendant stated in evidence that all the firing was done at night. Every morning the furnace was blocked so that it would not go ahead and melt. On the day, the inspector called, there was no annealing of bottles. The defendant was convicted and fined £6 together with £2 4s costs, being 27s 4d in each case, in default, imprisonment for seven days."

# Chapter 47

After helping in the reconstruction of the factory after the fire of 1897 Frank continued to work but as an employee. It took him many years to gain a discharge from his 1897 bankruptcy. Though never aired in public, Frank resented his treatment at the hands of his mother. It was Thomas who had forced them into many of the problems that plagued the business yet he had been tarred with the same brush. While Thomas had partied, he had been the constant hard working one. Many of the men had only stayed with the Ross's because they liked, respected and trusted this man who worked alongside them. After her husband's stroke Christina seemed to have blamed the conflict between her two eldest sons as the reason for Joseph's medical condition. She rarely spoke to them and seemed disinterested and dismissive of their opinions.

What had transpired with his brother Thomas, the court orders and bankruptcy, had altered Frank's personality. From a previously easy-going person who preferred working hands-on on the factory floor with the other glass blowers, trades men and boys, he became easily frustrated, prone to take offence at any time and for any reason. He had bouts of depression and would seem to sulk if he didn't get his own way. This resulted in a work environment where the least was said in an attempt to avoid conflict.

It is not surprising that Frank's son, James Clyde Ross, was the only grandchild who showed any interest in the business. James worked after school learning all aspects of the business and at only twelve and a half, he left school to work full time, starting when the factory was still located in Bray Street. James like his fellow workers was required to work from seven a.m. to five p.m. with a forty-five-minute lunch break and ten-minute afternoon break at three p.m. However, being a member of the family, he was expected to be at work by six thirty a.m. and not finish till the day's routine was done, regardless of the time. On many days this involved work late into the night. He didn't mind the long hours but the constant negative interaction with his uncle, Alexander, eventually forced him to leave. He gained a position as a carter but with the outbreak of World War One he joined the Australian Imperial Force (AIF) in October 1915. As he had three years as an army cadet in school and eighteen months in the Home Guard he joined as a lieutenant.

Frank Ross left the business in 1912 and the family moved to Derreleagh-Terrace, Gardeners Road, Mascot. The family then moved to Washington Street, West Kogarah. Much against the wishes of his wife, who saw it as an escape from the responsibilities, aged forty-two, Frank joined the army in December 1916 and served with the 45th Battalion Australian Imperial Expedition Force in France. In battle, he found himself required to charge out of the trenches that both sides had constructed, running across no-man's land. Men fell around him in hails of bullets, shrapnel and poison gas. He couldn't understand why they kept doing the same thing over and over as they were such easy target, but he followed orders. Life was miserable, the trenches were dirty, smelly and rampant with disease. Frank wore a scarf around his face to try and prevent his nostrils taking in the stench of stinking mud, open latrines, rotting corpses and unwashed bodies. It seemed to rain most days and the trenched flooded thus his woollen clothing were constantly wet and also smelt. Soldiers were not alone sharing their trenches with rats, frogs and lice. The nights were the worst, scared to sleep in case he became rat food. Mornings were no better as at day break the artillery shells would rain down or the enemy would launch their own attacks. One morning Frank woke, shivering and feeling dreadful. He had a high fever, severe headache, pain behind his eyes and soreness of leg and arm muscles. The medic called it trench fever, telling him it would pass in a few days. As it was transmitted by body lice, Frank was sent behind lines for treatment which included showering and fresh clothing. To him, being sent to the showers had been one of the highlights of the routine of war, as each tenth day men were allowed to go behind lines to have a shower. Here the men would strip, hand over their dirty clothing and be issued with a clean uniform. Small, medium or large, just pick the one that fitted you the best. Food in the trenches was limited, canned corn beef, bread, biscuits and some tea was the most they could expect. Everything was cold and the bread was terrible, made from ground turnips, and if there was meat, it was the poor horses that had been killed in battle.

It was almost a relief when he was gassed and suffered a shrapnel wound in the stomach, thus, after a stint in an army hospital, he was discharged. Though home the war never left him. His night terrors were often of the first person he had killed. A German charging towards his trench, the rifle shot that hit his enemy in the chest, the shocked look on the man's face as his body twisted and fell. The deep blue eyes like his son James, the youth must have been about the same age or even younger. Many nights the face was his son, and Frank would wake covered in sweat.

Following the war, he and his family were still living in Washington Street, West Kogarah, and with the support of his wife Frank opened a successful fish shop in Mortdale, a southern suburb of Sydney. The war had taken its toll with Frank, becoming more dependent on alcohol for relief from his inner pain.

Frank died in 1943 and was buried at Woronora Cemetery, Sutherland.

Frank's son, James Clyde Ross, was educated at the Arncliffe College, Arncliffe and after he left the bottle works, joined the army in 1916, age twenty-three, identifying himself as a general carrier and auctioneer.

He enlisted November 1915, initial training Holsworthy. In August of 1916 he left Australia on the *Kyarra*. James did not escape the risks of warfare but in his case it was influenza that ravaged the battlefields in Rouen, France that resulted in the end of his war in November 1916 and was evacuated to London on the hospital ship *Austurias*, from Havre. He remembered the ship with its white hull with a broad green band punctuated by a large red cross. He also remember the cold salt water baths and the smell of chloroform that came from the operating theatre. There were over eight hundred wounded soldiers and being an officer, his ward of eighty-five was the converted dining room. Though very ill and often struggling for breath, the doctors informed him he was fortunate as by their reckoning influenza had killed more soldiers than any one battle during the war. Discharged from London General Hospital February 1917, James returned to Australia on the *Benalla* and left the army in October 1917 as a second lieutenant, 18th Battalion, Australian Imperial Forces. He had received the 1914/15 Star, the British War

Medal and the Victory Medal. Just before leaving London, he was shocked to hear that despite being a clearly marked hospital ship, the *Austurias* had been torpedoed by a German U-boat with the loss of thirty-five lives.

Back in Sydney, James became a member of the All for Australia League (AFAL), an Australian political movement during the Great Depression founded in early 1931. Being a member of this organisation gave James some very influential contacts and support as the executive was strongly representative of managerial and professional men. They included: Major-General Gordon Bennett; Andrew Craig, treasurer of the Sydney Chamber of Commerce; Albert Heath, president of the Sydney and Suburban Timber Merchants' Association; Cecil Hoskins, chairman and managing director of Australian Iron and Steel; Sydney Snow, vice-president of the Retail Traders' Association; Alfred Bennett, manager of radio station 2GB; Sir Henry Braddon, member of the New South Wales Legislative Council; Charles M. McDonald, president of the New South Wales Employers' Federation and Mildred Muscio, feminist, representative of the women's committee.

The league was right-wing and anti-establishment in nature, and had the backing of a number of prominent businessmen and industrialists. It was critical both of the Labor Party and the right-wing Nationalist Party. It primarily operated in Sydney, but also had branches in country NSW and absorbed a similar organisation in Victoria. The league eventually chose to co-operate with the existing Nationalist organisation at the 1931 federal election, helping preselect candidates for the new United Australia Party (UAP). After the election victory the league was absorbed by the UAP's state organisation.

James became Member of the NSW Legislative Assembly as United Australia Party member for Kogarah from June 1939 to April 1941. He then rejoined the 2nd Australian Military Force during World War Two as a major.

After returning from the war, James made a living as a commercial traveller and clothing manufacturer but in retirement opened a winery in Lanhams Road, Winston Hills. The building had been part of the Old Toongabbie farm set up by Governor Phillip, the first governor of the New South Wales colony, in the eighteenth century. The building had formerly been used as a dairy farm then as a cheese factory.

# Chapter 48

As the Greek philosopher Plato stated, 'Everything changes and nothing stands still,' and so it was with most aspects of Christina's life. One cornerstone of her beliefs shifted when in 1902, five Methodist denominations in Australia, the Wesleyan Methodist Church, the Primitive Methodist Church, the Bible Christian Church, the United Methodist Free and the Methodist New Connection Churches came together to form a new church. This was to be called the Methodist Church of Australia. Christina though not actively involved in church administration, was supportive of the amalgamation. As a businesswoman, she understood the importance of the economy of scale. The duplication and competition between like bodies had always been a challenge for the Ross family in business. She knew that as far back as 1875, lay had representation in the churches and recently the role of women, though not equal, as accepted.

The combination of churches as a whole had seen a consistent growth with total Methodists in 1861 making up 6.2% of denominations but by 1901

10.2%. This had resulted from the evangelic activity of the lay leaders and the aggressive pioneer ministers in rural and remote regions of the colony.

The previous major divisions had a historical basis, a conflict with the tradition centralised authority where male ministers, through their Conferences, controlled all aspects of the church. The breakaway groups wanted more local control, greater involvement of lay people and certainly a greater say for women. Many were distressed that central judgements were often completely against the wishes of local congregations. In addition, between 1830 and 1890 society had become more literate, gained voting rights and become more socially aware and active.

This had driven her father to change his religious stance and also supported her own basic beliefs in an egalitarian society. However, she was a realist, and saw her beliefs as a political doctrine rather than a social philosophy. She believed that all people, convict, free settler, British or from some other part of the world should have the same political, economic, social and civil rights. This naturally also applied to the rights of women and their children. Again as a business woman, property owner and employer, she didn't want class warfare and realised it was impossible and actually undesirable to strive for complete economic egalitarianism. Yes, she wanted change, but to her this change needed to take the form of welfare for the needy and in certain legal reforms such as the rights of women in divorce.

# Chapter 49

Joseph died on the 23rd of July 1909 at his home at 70 Bray Street, Erskineville, aged 74. His will left all property to his wife Christina, except for his moulds and tools which he left to his son, John Ross. He also left fifty pounds to his daughter, Josephine Walker nee Ross. She had married Ernest Walker, even though Christina had expressed concerns regarding his character. Ernest, when aged twelve, had been sentenced to the *Vernon*, the same reformatory ship that Christina's son Joe had been on. Shortly after Earnest's arrival on the *Vernon* it was replaced by another ship, the *Sobraon*. As an adult, he was employed as a baker, and with their three children lived in one of Josephine's mothers investment properties. After Joseph's initial stroke Josephine had taken over the care of her father.

The hearse, a solid black carriage with etched glass sides stood outside their Bray Street house. Late in the morning, the cortège had moved toward the station. The four black horses decked out in silver with black plumes on their heads strained as the large wheels almost bounced over some of the larger cobblestones. There was also two mourning coach each with one horse and the family all in black walking solemnly behind. They were accompanied by many of the men and boys who worked in the factory, all decked out in their Sunday best.

Christina marvelled at the recently completed solid sandstone structure of the Regent Street mausoleum station. An ornate Victorian Free Gothic building with carved pillars with leafy capitals and Roman design. The sandstone angels, cherubs and gargoyles looked too impressive and beautiful to be wasted as a gathering point for grief ridden souls whose minds would be reflecting on the life of their lost ones. The station was one of two, the other the Necropolis Receiving Station within Rookwood was of equal splendour. For those who didn't know these as stations, they could mistake them as churches, both in structure and in the symbolic elements that adorned them.

Each day there would be several mourning groups that would join the eight-carriage train that carried coffins and family to final resting places. Once the large mourning parties boarded the train, it moved away at nine thirty a.m. in billows of black smoke for the eleven mile journey towards the Rookwood Cemetery. As the mourners sat in the carriages at the front, the coffins were at the rear in the hearse carriages. This consisted of a four-wheeled van that carried up to ten coffins on its upper and lower shelves. Each of the shelves were designed so they could be opened onto the platform. Christina noticed that at each station the train passed, those on the platforms would bow their heads or remove their hats as a sign of respect. After leaving the main line onto a spur they reached an equally impressive station building within the cemetery, each group of sad indistinct faces separated as each respective funeral trudged towards their allocated section of the large, seven hundred and eighty acre hectare (three hundred and fourteen hectare) cemetery. Protestant here, Greek Orthodox there, Catholic down the hill, Christina couldn't understand this need for separation, especially now when souls were supposedly already in heaven or hell. As she walked past the older graves she smiled at the Dillwynia, a shrub with a simple yellow flower and downy wattle also with its yellow blooms. It was nice to see something alive in this otherwise silent place.

On a gravestone, a round black granite column, in Rookwood Cemetery, Lidcombe NSW is the following family tribute:

"A tribute to the memory of Joseph Ross, the founder of the glass industry in Australia, having made the first pot of glass in Darling Harbour, Sydney 18th Aug. 1866."

The base was surrounded by four large chunks of glass, the last pouring from the glassworks furnace.

His death was announced in the *Sydney Morning Herald* on the 24th of July 1909:

"Death of Mr Joseph Ross.
Pioneer Glassblower of Australia.
The death took place yesterday, at his residence, Bray-Street. Erskineville, of Mr Joseph Ross, an old and well-known resident of Sydney. Mr Ross was the pioneer of the glass industry in Australasia, having mixed and smelted the first pot of glass, and made the first lot of bottles on August 18, 1866, at Darling Harbour, on the site now- occupied by the Fresh Food and Ice Company.

In founding the glass trade Mr Ross surmounted great difficulties. That he has left his mark is evinced by the fact that four of his sons are now engaged in this business. Mr Ross's first apprentice is the managing-director of the Melbourne Bottle Works; another apprentice is works manager of the Sydney Glass-works, whilst a third is carrying on business on his own account. Mr Ross took an active interest in municipal and political affairs and was one of the founders of the Chamber of Manufactures, being on the first council, and several times a delegate at interstate conferences. He was also one of the promoters of the Protection and Political Reform

League and was always an ardent advocate for protection to Australian industry.

As an employer of labour, he was respected by all his men. A proof of this is the fact that four of his employees were 38, 37, 36, and 35 years respectively in his service, whilst many others have served from 16 to 30 years.

He leaves a widow and a family of five sons and two daughters, the latter being Mrs Boag, of Newtown, and Mrs Walker, of Marrickville. Mr Ross was born in Sunderland, England, in 1830, of Scottish parents."

# Chapter 50

Christina died on the 14th of June 1914 at her home, 70 Bray Street, Erskineville, aged seventy-two. She was buried in the Methodist section of the Rookwood cemetery. Her daughter Christina Boag and the family's chartered accountant William Chapman were shown as the joint trustees for the will of Christina Ross.

*The Daily Telegraph*, Sydney, 15th of June 1914 carried the announcement:

"An Old Pioneer, Death of Mrs Ross.

Mrs Christina Ross, widow of the late Mr Joseph Ross— the pioneer glass manufacturer of Australia— died early yesterday morning at her residence, Bray Street, Erskineville. Deceased was born in Edinburgh, Scotland, in 1841. In the sixties she was of very valuable assistance to her husband in establishing the glass industry, and for many years she made all the clay pots or crucibles in which the raw materials for making glass were smelted. Mrs Ross had a large family, of whom four sons and two daughters are alive, as well as about 30 grandchildren. The eldest son, Thomas Ross, is the director of Vance and Ross, Ltd., glass bottle manufacturers, and he is an ex-Mayor of Waterloo, senior vice-president, of the South Sydney Hospital, and a member of the council of the Chamber of Manufactures. Mr Frank Ross is in business on his own account; whilst John and Alexander Ross are members of the firm of Ross Bros., glass bottle makers. The daughters, Mrs Boag and Mrs Walker, are well-known residents of Newtown and Erskineville, Mrs Ross was a very old member of the Methodist Church. The funeral will take place to-day in the Methodist portion of the Necropolis, Rookwood."

Christina Boag nee Ross, was living in a home owned by her mother at 31 Bray Street near the Ross Brothers glass works. Christina, Joseph's and Christina's third daughter, had married James Allen Boag in 1895. At the time, he was working as a foreman in the glassworks but after Joseph sold his business, he gained employment with the Australian Gaslight Company. Eventually, with his wife Christina running his business, he had become a successful plumber on the north shore. The couple had three children, Alexander who died as an infant, James Fraser and Herbert Allen. Christina was very much like her mother, the same controlled and clinical temperament. Unbeknown to her brothers, the two women over the years had held many long conversations about family and the business. Both had agreed that John would be the most suitable to run the factory, he had his father's level of skills and like his brother Frank, got on well with the men. On the other hand Alexander was strong-willed and rather arrogant. The men didn't react well to his autocratic leadership style and both women were concerned that several key workers would leave if he gained permanent control.

John and Alexander both resented the Boag's involvement in what they saw as their business, again leading to another set of combatants within the family.

# Chapter 51

One of Christina's grandsons had been walking home from school when he noticed a commotion taking place ahead of him. A crowd was gathering, so like all children he was excited with expectation, but shocked when he realised it was one of the Ross firm's six horse drawn wagons ablaze outside Grace Brothers department store on Parramatta Road. They had managed to disconnect the horses but red blue flames danced high into the air as the sounds of exploding bottles made both the firemen and spectators wary. The heat was intense, with this main thoroughfare to the west blocked in both directions. The commotion was made worse by the hundreds of shoppers and store assistant rushing out of the five-storey department store as smoke swirled into open windows causing many to think the building itself was on fire.

In a rush to get the finished bottles to market, still hot bottles were packed and had ignited the straw used to line the wooden packing crates on the wagon. At the time, there was unprecedented demand for Ross products as the world war meant Australia now had to support its own domestic market plus supply the demand for glass containers in New Zealand, Pacific Islands, Malaya, Hong Kong, Japan, China and Hawaii.

Prior to her death, Christina had been aware of the impending, though geographically removed, danger to her and her family. Wearing her ever-thickening spectacles, she had maintained her interest in world events and scanned the newspaper for details about what she considered convoluted and fragmented governance at national and international levels. To the end of her life, she enjoyed debates with her inner circle of friends and where some women discussed fashion, food or knitting she preferred talking of nationalism, imperialism, alliances and militarism. Always concerned how these growing world issues affected business and families. She felt that the concepts of territorial and economic competition at a world level were really no different to the challenges that the Ross business had faced for years, trying to keep and expand their market. She and Joseph had revelled when a competitor went under and had faced this harsh reality several times themselves. Joseph had called their challenges Social Darwinism, where only the fittest deserved to survive. He had always believed he was the best and challenged his family to follow the same mantra.

At the outbreak of war, the First Australian Imperial Force (AIF) was the Army's main expeditionary force and had been formed on the 15th of August 1914 with an initial strength of twenty-thousand men, following Britain's declaration of war on Germany. Meanwhile, the separate, hastily raised two thousand-man Australian Naval and Military Expeditionary Force landed near Rabaul in German New Guinea on the 11th of September 1914 and obtained the surrender of the German garrison after ten days.

The AIF initially consisted of one infantry division and one light horse brigade. The first contingent had departed Australia by ship for Egypt on the 1st of November 1914, where it formed part of the Australian and New Zealand Army Corps (ANZAC). Following the armistice on the 11th of November 1918, a process of demobilisation began, with the last Australian personnel being repatriated in late 1919. In all, four hundred and sixteen thousand eight hundred and nine Australians enlisted during the war and three hundred and thirty four thousand served overseas. The AIF sustained approximately two hundred and ten thousand casualties, of which sixty-one thousand five hundred and nineteen were killed or died of wounds, a casualty rate among the highest of any.

For the Ross's and other glass manufacturers, the war created a boom rather than bust. Unlike many other industries, their market was predominantly local, and most were of a scale that the inflow from overseas was not essential for their businesses. Raw materials were also local thus they were not cut off from vital imports like others. As essential workers, their factories were considered exempt and unlike other countries, conscription had not been introduced in Australia, South Africa or India. All the Australians who fought in World War One were volunteers. With federation in 1901, the 1903 Defence Act stated, "Unless they voluntarily agreed to do so." The country had held two conscription referenda, 1916 and 1917, but both times the population voted "no" to the Labour Prime Minister Billy Hughes requests.

What might be seen as a positive was the war also saw Joseph's hopes for greater protection of Australian industries eventuate. In 1921 the so-called "Greene Tariff" was introduced with wide-ranging revision of tariff schedules carried out by the Customs Minister, Sir Walter Greene. Many of the industries that had developed during the war period were less efficient than their overseas counterparts and would have failed if free trade would have resumed. The war had also made Australians realise the importance of reducing their dependency on overseas suppliers.

On a personal note, members of the Ross family had taken an active role in the war, volunteering in defence of their country. Though his wife openly said that he was running away from his responsibilities, Christina's son Frank served in the 45th Battalion Australian Imperial Expedition Force, wounded and gassed in Europe, his life would never be the same.

Frank's son, James Clyde Ross, was a warrant officer in the 18th Battalion and also fought in Europe as did Thomas Ross's sons, Thomas Ross a lance corporal in the 8th Australian Field Ambulance, Imperial Force, and Frederick Ross a sergeant in the 3rd Division Cyclist Company AIF. Cyclists in the 1st and 2nd Divisions were used as dispatch riders but the 3rd didn't see any action, being disbanded on arrival in England and assigned to administrative duties. For these younger men, their reasons for joining varied. For some it was their duty to the British Empire, "the mother country", that had been ground into them during their schooling, while for others it was a chance to escape from the drudgery of normal life. Perhaps they all saw it as a great adventure with bonds of friendship, being paid to travel to places they may otherwise could never afford to go.

As the war dragged on and the published lists of dead and wound grew the reason to join became more sober. Men began to feel guilty or shamed by others that they has remained in the relative safety of essential industries and farm output. Associated with these losses was the realisation it was now essential to win the war at any cost, a war that they had been told in the heady days of 1914 would be 'over by Christmas.'

Fortunately, all serving Ross men returned.

# Chapter 52

The fight for control of the family business reached another crisis point when Alexander Ross took legal action against his sister Christina Boag and accountant, William Chaplin. Alexander resented the fact that though it was he, and his brother John, who were running the factory, their mother had not trusted then with its control. Even though John was four years older, Alexander had also previously been disappointed when his father's will had left all the businesses tools and moulds to John, so now felt even greater resentment that he had not been appointed receiver and manager of Ross Brothers. He vocally aired his grievances to anyone who would listen, questioning why his sister and Chaplin deserved to be paid significant management fees.

John was more accepting of his parents' actions, and though appearing to publicly support Alexander, realised that if the business was going to survive there was a need to modernise to remain competitive. Walking the fine line between the two warring sides he brokered sufficient consensus to allow plans to be drawn up to expand and mechanise the business.

Tenders were called for the supply and installation of a glass blowing machine and the business advertised for new staff. Up till then all Ross bottles were individually mouth blown and hand finished with a lipping tool.

John had read about the developments that had occurred overseas in the mechanisation of bottle making. From 1890 on, semiautomatic machines had been in use in Europe and America and though largely displacing hand blowers, they still required specialist skilled workers to run, and only produced a limited range. Because of Australia's small domestic market, this machine had not been suitable, as high volume was not the Ross's major market. Their market was providing a smaller number of an extensive range of drink, pharmaceutical and food bottles and jars, addressing on-demand needs.

From about 1905, the Owens automatic machine was available and though it greatly reduced the need for skilled labour, the capital outlay was high and following the depression of the 1890s confidence in the future of the colony's industrial sector was not strong. When John was considering mechanisation in 1920 the trade had been revolutionised by the introduction of feed and flow devices.

Gaining agreement between his warring siblings with their bouts of no-talks and baseless accusations seem to take forever. Eventually, self-interest won the day, as regardless of individual motives, each wanted and needed the business to succeed. At the final hurdle, fate was to deal a ruinous hand, with the factory again severely damaged by fire. The building was gutted, and stock destroyed. As a result, the coal dealer, Jones Brothers, took the Ross Brothers to court to get payments of seven hundred and fifty pounds worth of coal owed to them. As the registered owners, Christina and William took the case to the Supreme Court but lost.

Realising the business was in trouble, John Ross and his younger sister, Josephine Waterhouse nee Ross, took the Ross Brothers business to court as creditors in an attempt to gain their share of their mother's estate. The court ruled in their favour, resulting in the Erskineville business being wound up.

John Ross who was living at 72 Bray Street in one of his mother's original investment houses, attempted to establish his own glassworks but due to technical difficulties it did not open. As his skills were limited to glass manufacturing, he gained employment with the Australian Glass Manufactures as a general hand. He never married and developed tuberculosis, dying in his Rawson Street home, Granville, 1949.

So ended Christina's and Joseph's glass legacy. From their first bottle made in Darling Harbour in 1866 to the last Ross glassworks closing in 1922, this pioneering family had seen their new homeland change from a penal colony to a country of envied lifestyle. They had faced recessions and war, bankruptcy and boom. Between them they had fought for the rights of local industry and rights for women. The Ross family, like so many families who had taken the challenge to forge a better life, had become a cornerstone of the Australian economy.

As with so many industries, the time of the artisan working in small family craft-based businesses had ended. By the 1920s, the Australian Glass Manufacturers (AGM) had become the monopoly in glassmaking in Sydney. This had been achieved through the amalgamation of smaller manufacturers such as the Waterloo Glass Bottle Works Ltd, Vance and Ross, the Zetland Glass Bottle Works and the Melbourne Glass Bottle Works Co Ltd. In 1926 AGM was to form a subsidiary, Crown Crystal Glass Pty Ltd, producing crystal as well as cut and blown glassware for industrial and household use, including Pyrex.

# Chapter 53

So, what remains of Christina's legacy?

Like so many women in the pages of history, Christina was allocated a secondary role, marginalised by her gender.

In the *Australian Dictionary of Biography*, she was relegated to the person at least early in the marriage, who made the clay pots and crucibles. There was also a passing reference to her owning the house in which they lived. However, in the *Encyclopaedia of Australian Science and Innovation*, she does not rate a mention at all, nor is she recognised in the *Academy of Technological Sciences and Engineering's*, "Technology in Australia 1788—1988."

In the *Australian Society* newsletter April 1979, on glass companies in NSW, the only mention was "Christina, wife of Joseph Ross, died aged 73." Similar appears in a 1870s article in the *Queanbeyan Age*, a regional newspaper, referring to the Ross crucibles being of highly serviceable character, calling them "products of colonial industry." The article praises Mr Ross for making everything in the factory "himself". Again, the contribution of women to colonial industrial development was ignored.

Society in the late 1800s and into the twentieth century saw women like Christina having a chief role and value in terms of that as a wife and mother. Women were expected to be passive, gentle and caring. Christina, like many of her peers, was not thought to be equal to men and had been denied many of the same rights and opportunities.

Like many of her gender, their legacy partly lies in their descendants, who encompass an extensive range of professions and community involvement. However, if known at all, Christina is simply a name in their heritage chart or a listing on an ancestry web site.

Joseph's epitaph failed to recognise her contribution or even name her: "He left a wife…" Her own epitaph in *The Daily Telegraph*, Sydney, 15th of June 1914 only made mention of her "very valuable assistance to her husband," but focussed on the traditional values of motherhood and the achievements of her sons. While Joseph's funeral was held on a large scale with pomp and ceremony, Christina's was a simple graveside service attended by family and a few close friends.

There is of course the marble column that stands in Rookwood cemetery, honouring Joseph and Christina. However, the inscription reads: "A tribute to the memory of Joseph Ross, the founder of the glass industry in Australia." As if to add insult to omission, sadly with time comes disrespect and the irreplaceable poured glass base has been smashed and stolen by vandals.

For the collector of Australian history, there are the bottles and jars of all shapes, sizes and uses that antique sellers offer at premium prices, some for thousands of dollars. Again, the books that do refer to Ross bottles also fail to elaborate on Christina's contribution.

Christina was a strong and talented woman, mother and entrepreneur, who used her networking, media and financial skills to support her family and the family business. Like so many pioneering women, she did exceptional things, living a fascinating life as someone willing to challenge the accepted norms of nineteenth century society. Perhaps the most significant reminder of this determined pioneer is this, her story, without which, her amazing endeavours would be lost.

Like her grandmother, Barbara Sinclair, Christina had recognised societies injustices had chosen to fight the fact that she had fewer rights in law including not being able to vote, even though she eventually owned considerable property. Though personally reluctant to verbalise her feelings and achievements to any but her closest friends and daughter, we should not be willing to accept that any Ross story should be "his story", another white, elite and male history. Though Joseph

Ross was an industrial pioneer in his own right, it was Christina's drive and business acumen that created a lasting legacy.

www.ingramcontent.com/pod-product-compliance
Lightning Source LLC
Chambersburg PA
CBHW040520170726
48295CB00012B/279